...from Ba

…from Barcelona

Stories Behind The City: Volume 1

Jeremy Holland

NativeSpain.™com

First Published in 2009 by
Native Spain (www.nativespain.com)

Typeset in Book Antiqua

Cover photograph © Copyright Daniel Flower
www.flickr.com/photos/danielflower
danielflower@gmail.com

*To all aspiring artists – Remember
it's a marathon and the tortoise wins.*

Acknowledgements

If you're reading this, thank you.

This book would not be possible without the support of Debbie Jenkins and everybody at Lean Marketing Press who took a chance on an unknown author and an untested idea. Let's hope it's the start of a beautiful and successful friendship!

A special thanks to the editors, Sharon Brown for the unenviable task of doing the line edit and all her useful suggestions during the final stages and Ira Shull for his invaluable comments and advice while writing the stories. Like every man needs a good woman so does every author need a good editor and you are two of the best.

To my beautiful wife Guillermina whose patience and understanding throughout this endeavor would put Job to shame and to my baby girl Elisenda who has brought daddy nothing but good fortune. Also, as I promised ten years ago should this day ever arrive, to my dear friend Jay Askinos who encouraged me to write when all I did was talk about it. When are you going to dust off the pen, pisha?

Finally, last but definitely not least, to the wonderful people and the beautiful city of Barcelona, muchisimas gracias for the inspiration and the stories. I could not have chosen a better place to make my adoptive home - *un beso muy enorme por todo*.

Jeremy Holland
November 2009

Praise

"Ten colorful and unique stories about Barcelona written by an expat author with his finger on the pulse of the city. He manages to capture both the vitality and the mysteriousness of the capital of Catalunya in a fresh and entertaining way."

Carlos Carbonell, ADN Newspaper, Barcelona

"Enjoyable, well-written and entertaining stories for everyone from the tourist to the expat to the native. Recommended for distant lovers of Barcelona like myself and locals too!"

Bart Van Poll, founder, Spotted by Locals Cityblogs

"A must read, must have for tourists and expats alike. Every story is fascinating. You'll get so much more out of your stay than from an infoseek guide book. I'm impatiently waiting for volume two!"

Rosie Reay, author, book critic, Catalunya Chronicle

"These compelling stories move at a cracking pace, led by realistic characters, who move and act in scenes that evoke both the Barcelona I know and one I most certainly don't."

**Jo Parfitt, author of twenty-four books
including A Moving Landscape**

"Having lived in Barcelona for four years, I was looking for a book that shows the real city. The realism of the characters puts you in the skin of someone living there as you experience the love-hate relationship many locals have and live the absurd and funny situations that only seem to happen there."

Alejandro Conty, Sony Studios, Alice in Wonderland

Foreword

To get to know a city you need to absorb its language, its culture, its history and its fiction. A city like Barcelona is no different. Speaking as someone who spent a week there sightseeing just six months ago, the Barcelona I know is the one from the Dorling Kindersley Top Ten series. Do I truly know the city? Not a chance.

As a linguist, a writer and someone who has lived and worked in five countries myself, I like to get to really know the places in which I live and also those I visit as a tourist. However, getting to know the real Paris, the real Rome or the real Barcelona, is difficult until you live there and mix, work and speak with the locals. This book puts you on the fast track to the inside story behind the city.

Here, in this collection of short stories, American Jeremy Holland introduces us to a Barcelona that is beyond the guide books, beneath the surface and that shows us not only the current city but also allows us a glimpse into its past. It is through these stories that we come to understand the importance of St George and the Dragon and why the patron saint of England came to be the inspiration for Gaudí's Casa Batlló. We learn the reality of the famous Las Ramblas, and how at night, it's home to the other Barcelona of prostitutes and transsexuals. How the glorious, historic Gothic Quarter made famous by Picasso in Les Demoiselles d'Avignon becomes a dark playground for drunken tourists and drug dealers. It is through these pages that we can get under the skin of the stunning city and meet its people - from the sultry, dark beauties, to the unshaven old men propping up the bars to the locals trapped in the rat race, frustrated by bureaucracy and affected by the souring economy.

Is this, then, the real Barcelona? Is this an insight into the reality of life for the locals – Catalans and expatriates who live, work, love, commute, have affairs and break the law there? The pickpockets, the overcrowded metro, the political corruption, the unwanted tourists, the illegal workforce, the crime. All are here in stark juxtaposition to the glorious work of Antoni Gaudí, el Palau de la Música, Casa Milà, Montjuïc and Parc Güell.

These compelling stories move at a cracking pace, led by realistic characters, who move and act in scenes that evoke both the Barcelona I know and one I most certainly don't. Bookended between two compelling stories written, unusually, in the second person so the reader can step into another world. Now, thanks to this book, I think I understand.

Not only do these stories inspire and inform the reader, but they also provoke and add a piquancy to the capital of Catalunya that will make any long or short-term visitor stop and think.

As a writer and one who is addicted to travel, I commend this collection of stories for enriching my view of this fine city and letting me get under its skin.

Jo Parfitt
www.joparfitt.com

Contents

First Impressions

The guidebook says the heart of Barcelona is Las Ramblas and El Barrio Gotico. To save on the cost of a taxi, you take the metro from the hotel. It's the middle of August and all the hot air trapped in the tunnels makes it feel like the inside of a sauna; a leaky faucet drips on the burning coals producing nothing but waves of steam. To take your mind off the heat, you stare at the digital clock hanging from the low ceiling. *Proper Tren 3:04*, it says. From the little Spanish you know, "*proximo*" is the word for "next" and "*propio*" is "own". Intrigued by this linguistic puzzle, you decide that this train must be a "proper" or a *real* train, which stops at all the stations, as opposed to an express service like in your home town of New York City. It's a perfectly logical theory.

On the opposite platform sits a dark Spanish girl in a loose white dress on a metal bench. Even from this distance, she has a relaxed and natural beauty, making her far prettier than the model on the poster next to her. Trying unsuccessfully not to stare, you wonder if there might be a romantic liaison on this vacation and imagine chatting up such a gorgeous woman. The girl makes eye contact and holds it a second, giving the possibility a slight hope. A sleek train approaches with a gust of wind that dries the beading sweat. It squeals to a stop and blocks the view. The doors beep open and close. The train rumbles to a start and leaves. The platform is empty; the girl is gone.

The clock says, *Proper Tren 1:08*. People descend the stairs on either side of your platform and come to a stop. A few push through to the less populated middle section. More Spanish girls appear. Dressed in summer tank-tops and short shorts, they are all petite with nice round curves and walk with a sexy swish that girls back home seem to lack. They are all cute enough to turn a quick peek into a double-take, although none are as attractive as the girl in the white dress.

The sweat returns. You wipe it away with the back of the arm, look up and notice that the deadly third rail is above the tracks unlike in New York City where it's on the ground. The metal rail vibrates. Another refreshing blast of wind blows through. The tunnel lights up. The clock shows 00:05. The first car whizzes by. The entire chain of five, older and more box-shaped cars to a screeches to a stop. The clock says, *ENTRA*. High-pitched beeps sound. The metal handles on the doors turn up. People rush out and shove you to the side, making you feel back at home.

A boy in Bermuda shorts is the last to leave and, at his exit, you enter. A rattling air-conditioner blows out warm air as you squeeze through tight openings between standing passengers looking for some space to stand. Two back-packers, carrying something that looks like it belongs on a mountain expedition stop the progress. Six foot is the average height in the states, but here it feels tall and you look over the heads of the brown Spaniards and make eye-contact with the fellow, sun-kissed tourists as the train heads to the next station: Plaça Catalunya.

***

2

The metro stops and the entire car empties. The majority of exiting passengers turn right and shuffle down the platform, up a set of stairs and through automatic sliding doors, before heading down a white passageway with a ceiling that just clears your head. At the end two women kneel behind cloths displaying lighters for sale and directly across is a bright bar enclosed in glass where a single patron drinks a beer under a clock that reads 10:00 a.m. Radiohead sung in a husky voice to an out of tune guitar bounces off the stone walls. Turning the corner, you see it belongs to a boy in camouflage pants who stands in the middle of a bright green mosaic surrounded by gray walls. Commuters toss coins in his dusty cap and rush towards the glass doors of the metro entrance or up and down two sets of steps. It's as dizzyingly busy as the 42nd Street subway station in downtown Manhattan but a tenth of the size. A bronze sign that says, "Las Ramblas" shows you the way out.

As the escalator rises from the dim underground to a bright surface, your eyes blink and adjust to the new scene. Elegant stone buildings with iron balconies overlook tall green trees shading a pedestrian promenade. Honking cars and revving scooters zoom down two narrow one-way streets on either side of the rose-shaded pavement. Thousands of tourists speaking in multiple languages come from all directions. The noise and people bombard your brain and short circuit the decision making process, frying any ability to think or react as the crowd sweeps you up like a river's current and takes you down Barcelona's most famous street - Las Ramblas.

A man covered in a thick white paint sits on a toilet atop a wooden box. The humidity seeps through your clothes and sticks to the skin. Chirps that sound more like cries come from blue stands selling caged animals.

The window of a red newsstand displays a mustard and crimson striped flag with the figure of a black and white donkey. Flapping the shirt to cool down, you think about U.S. politics and wonder if there's a Democratic party here. The view ahead reveals nothing but a haze of thousands of people, vendor stands and trees for what seems like miles into the distance. It's worse than Times Square. You spot a restaurant advertising air-conditioning and decide to take a break from the heat and eat something before continuing the sightseeing.

Coming in from the muggy outside makes the cold air of the place feel arctic. The lights are bright and the floor is alternating black and white tiles. A metal railing divides a dining section of wooden tables and chairs from a metallic counter with stools, making it look more like a cafeteria than a dining establishment. There are few diners and only a Pakistani waiter works the main section. Behind the bar is a young Chinese boy and you realize, just like in most major cities, Barcelona has immigrants working in their restaurants. You take a seat at the counter and ask, "What you got for breakfast?"

The Chinese boy points to a single croissant and a pack of donuts under a glass case.

"Any eggs?"

"Yes. We have eggs."

"And bacon?"

"Yes. *Plato combinado* number fou'." He points to a poster-size menu on the wall behind the bar. The menu items are written in Spanish and another language that looks a bit like French.

"Okay. One of those."

"To drink?"

"Orange juice and coffee."

4

"You want coffee *now*?" His statement causes the Pakistani waiter to pause and look.

"Yes."

You check out the other customers to see what *faux pas* has been committed. A family speaks German over baguettes and bottles of soda at a table by the window with a view of the street. Near them two Spanish women talk loudly over small cups of coffee, cigarettes and empty plates. Even pushing forty, they have a Latin sultriness to them making your stare linger just a little bit longer than normal. They catch you, make eye contact and smile.

"You wan' *thoomo natural* or bo'le?" asks the waiter breaking the moment.

You turn away from the women and reply, "Natural, please," before looking back to see them paying to leave.

They give you another look and smile but nothing more, as they stand and walk out the door. Your focus shifts back to the waiter as he clicks the button on a green machine. A wheel lifts the oranges up and down into an extractor that pours the juice into a metal jug. Next, he goes to an espresso maker and prepares the coffee before heading to the kitchen.

Five minutes later he returns with the complete order. "Here you go."

In front of you sits a *café con leche*, which is a 'cafe latte' served in something closer in size to a teacup than the soup bowl that passes for an American mug. The freshly squeezed orange juice is what looks like a champagne glass on a saucer with a pack of sugar and a small spoon. According to the menu on the wall, *Plato combinado no. 4* is *ous fregits, beicon i patates fregides / huevo frito, beicon y patatas fritas*. On a white plate between the juice and coffee are two fried eggs, two strips of bacon, and a handful of fries.

"Ketchup?" enquires the waiter.

"No, thanks," you reply sawing at the tough bacon. "Just pepper."

***

The simple, yet overpriced meal leaves your stomach full. You appreciate the cold air for the last time by the door before returning to the heat and humidity of the outside. A row of parked scooters lean right and block the way across the one-way street. From this perspective, Las Ramblas seems to consist solely of the backs of blue and red vendor stands and rainbow-colored human statues spaced between thin gray trunks and spindly branches of the trees. Thousands of tourists blend into a single organism and in the glass doors that overlook it all signs advertise short-term apartments, language schools or tattoo parlors. Along the less congested sidewalk, large window panes display *I heart Barcelona* t-shirts, Mexican sombreros and football jerseys. Menus advertise paella, tapas and sangria. A revolving wooden door occasionally announces the existence of a five-star hotel. The scenery follows this pattern until you reach an arcade with a set of steps leading to *El Barrio Gotico* - the center of Barcelona's old city.

Five-story medieval buildings on either side shade and cool the narrow cobblestone street. More shop windows populate the ground level, although now displaying higher quality items such as decorative fans, elaborate scarves and dresses and the finest Spanish swords and leather. The green wooden shutters of the surrounding apartments above are closed; the only sign of life, a random potted plant, bicycle or a clothes rack left behind the rusted black railings of balconies. They don't have neighborhoods this old back in the states except for Indian burial grounds, making you stop and appreciate the history.

The name of a restaurant written in golden letters against a green background rings a bell. Pulling out your guidebook, flipping through the pages, you stop at the appropriate section and see that the name is circled. Through the open front door diners are squashed between a bar and the wall, forcing them to eat and drink with their arms tucked in like wings. It looks like your stomach feels - uncomfortable.

The street is crowded with shoppers and tourists, so you dip down the first side alley to do some solo exploring. An approaching crew of loud Italians in designer sunglasses requires another right, and then a left to avoid precarious scaffolding. As you journey deeper, the air grows darker and cooler. The distance between the smooth soot stained buildings is barely wider than an office corridor and there are no windows at the ground level – only closed metal shutters, simple aluminum doors and a piles of trash. Midway down the alley, a droopy string spans two balconies and holds a worn cloth with a picture of a crossed-out stick-figure taking a leak. This is not an image found in the guidebook. You are lost in Barcelona and New York City becomes nothing but a distant memory as your vacation truly begins.

Listening to nothing but gut instinct to escape the maze of streets, you veer left when the alley splits into a Y. Blooming flowers and lush plants hang from the balcony railings and offer a stark contrast to the worn and blackened stones. An intergalactic battle scene sprayed painted on a closed metal shutter announces the end of this tiny street, presenting another choice of left or right. The gut says right and you wander the web of centuries-old alleys where names like *Carrer Templers* and *Carrer Pi* appear in black Roman letters on marble plaques, the names evoking thoughts of a different era when knights walked these streets and secret societies met behind closed doors.

***

The smudged window of an antique bookstore seems like a good place to stop and rest your throbbing feet. The low clearance of the door causes you to duck and the wooden beam at the bottom makes the first step down feel like a drop. Inside, the air is heavy and stale in the dusky light. Ceiling-high shelves are crammed with what appear to be ancient treatises mixed in among worn paperbacks. A folding table by the windowsill contains stacks of brown stained maps and books of black and white photos, while at the back, a pile of papers on a glass desk moves with the breeze from an unseen fan. A thin man with flowing gray hair on the sides of an otherwise bald head appears from a dark room. His cloudy blue eyes narrow as his round glasses slip down his long nose. "*J-es,*" he says in accented English.

"I'm just looking around," you reply. "You have a lot of interesting books here."

"Yes. This is a bookstore. But I only have in Spanish and Catalan. Do you know Catalan?"

"Um, no, I'm just visiting."

Peering inquisitively as if you are an extraterrestrial scout sent to Barcelona on a reconnaissance mission, he comes around the desk and picks a random book from the shelf. He holds up the leather cover, points to the title and says, "*This* is Catalan."

The embroidered gold letters read: *Senyor Jordi i el Drac.*

"Is it about Dracula?" you ask.

"No! This title is *in* Catalan. It's the language of *Catalunya*!"

"Oh. What's it about?"

"St. George and the dragon: Our patron saint."

"Isn't that the same saint as England?"

"Yes, and the country of Georgia." He digs something from his nostril and flicks it to the ground. "You must be American."

"What makes you say that?"

"You have no sense of history. No one in the United States knows about *Catalunya*. We were a great empire. We sailed the Mediterranean and conquered Sardinia!"

"I didn't know that. Then again, I don't even know the fifty states." The man's upper lip curls in disgust at your ignorance. "What happened? Did Spain conquer you guys?" you say hoping to win him over with interest in this apparently important topic of *Catalunya*.

"No. The King of Aragón married the Queen of *Castilla* in 1469 uniting the Iberian Peninsula, except Portugal." He pauses and asks, "Where you from?"

"New York City."

"New York! Did you know that September 11th is our national day? It's when we celebrate losing the Spanish War of Succession in 1714."

"No, I didn't."

"Yes. It's a tragic date, no?"

"Yep."

He asks, "Do you know Barcelona?"

You reply, "It's my first day."

He stops and thinks again. "There's a good Catalan restaurant near here. You must try it."

"Does it serve those little pieces of bread with fish?"

"What?" His face wrinkles in deep thought at the question. "No. Those are *pintxos* from the Basque country."

"Oh."

"Come on, follow me. I show you where it is."

***

Outside, the sun once again makes an appearance and casts a rosy sheen on the buildings on one side of the street. The side with the bookshop remains covered by a dusty shadow as the man turns the sign in the window to *Tancat*, locking the door. He firmly takes your arm. "Come on. Let's go."

Walking at a quick pace that explains his trim figure, he navigates the twisting and meandering streets like someone who has grown up here. Even more lost and confused than before, your brain shuts down as you follow him like a mindless zombie until he finally stops at an open door next to a window.

He smiles and says, "Here we are."

The lingering discomfort in your stomach makes you ask, "*Dónde esta el baño?*"

"Eh?"

"The toilet!"

"Oh, *el lavobo*," he replies. "At the far back."

***

Inside the restaurant, a thick, musky mist of frying oil clings to your skin like humidity as you sprint under low wooden beams that brush the hair. At the back is a sink and two doors labeled *Homes* and *Dones*. Instinct says the former and you push the door to enter. It bangs against the toilet bowl and stops, leaving a space of six inches. It's a tight fit, but your body contorts and twists through the crack. Finally squeezing all the way inside, you press the button for the light. A ticking sounds. Your stomach gurgles. It's a struggle to turn around and bend down in such a small space. The rim of the toilet lacks any plastic, so you take some thin paper and wipe the porcelain. Breakfast will wait no longer and you squat. The ticking stops and the timed light cuts.

***

The man from the bookshop sits at the end of the bar by a smudged window with a blurry view of the stone building across the alley. He chats with a smoking bartender and starts laughing. "What?" you say.

"I have seen that green look many times. You aren't used to so much oil to cook food."

"What do you mean?"

"In the United States you cook everything with butter. That's why you are all so fat."

"No we don't. We use Pam."

"What's that?"

"A spray for pans."

The man has no idea what you're talking about. "Anyway, it's not like Mexico. You will feel better in a day."

"Okay."

"Listen, I must go now. My wife will kill me if I'm not home for lunch. Jordi will take good care of you."

"Do you live close?"

He stands and laughs at such an apparently stupid question. "Only immigrants and foreigners live in the Gothic Quarter. I live outside Barcelona and away from the noise and stress."

"I see. Well, thanks for everything."

He asks, "How do you say *de nada* in English?"

"You're welcome."

"In Catalan it's *De res*."

You ask, "How do you say 'goodbye' in Catalan?"

"*Adéu,*" he replies and walks out the door.

Alone with the bartender, you look around and take in the surroundings. Unlike the bright restaurant on Las Ramblas, this place is dark and small with white stone walls and a gray tiled floor. Hanging from the ceiling are thick, spotted, blood-sausages whose large sizes must make them the pythons of the sausage family. The smallest are burnt crimson, long and slender, while the shorter and fatter ones are black and white and the size of a loaf of French bread. Next to them dangles a carved pig's leg from its hoof. Staring at the red meat streak with white lines, you wonder if that's where the tough Spanish bacon comes from. "You eat?" asks the bartender, putting his tobacco stained fingers into his mouth to make sure you understand.

The stomach, still uncomfortable from breakfast, says no, but wanting to be an adventurous tourist, you say, "Yes," and scan the menu propped against the wall for a sandwich. *Tortilla* is the third choice and seems like a safe option.

"Beer to drink?" The bartender points at the brass tap with *Estrella* written on it.

"*Si, gracias.*"

He beams at your attempt at Spanish, revealing a set of five gray teeth as he takes a small glass goblet and fills it to the top.

***

A *tortilla* in Spain is not made of flour or corn but is instead a wedge of an inch-thick, round omelet lightly browned on top, with sliced fried-potatoes and chopped onions inside. The salty flavors please your taste buds, but an unsteady stomach protests at the ingredients. A gulp of the golden beer soothes the discomfort. The bartender leans against the bar, smokes, and watches a flat-screen TV above the door. On it is the most hideous woman that you've ever seen. "Who's that?"

"*La Duquesa de Alba.*" He looks disappointedly at the food sitting hardly touched on the plate. "You don't like?"

"No, no. I like it. I had breakfast earlier and I'm not hungry."

His blank expression reveals that he hasn't comprehended a word.

"More beer?" He points to the empty glass.

"No thanks. Just the check."

Again he looks lost. You trace an imaginary check in the air. He shows his five teeth to demonstrate understanding.

***

Once again outside, the alley remains cool and shaded. To the left, it leads back into the shadowy labyrinth that is *El Barrio Gotico* and the closed bookstore. To the right, there's a wall of light. Tired from all the exploring and walking, you decide it's time to meet some people, the best outcome being a pretty Spanish girl like the one in the white dress from the metro. The surrounding darkness lifts and the temperature rises as the alley comes to an abrupt stop at a concrete square under a hot sun.

A church from the Middle Ages stands on one side and looks like the perfect place to stay cool and get some culture before looking for traveling companions. The imposing walls are made of a smooth stone and rise at least five stories. There's little in the way of decoration and it's almost utilitarian, compared to the sharp spires and intricate carvings of the more famous Gothic Cathedral from the cover of the travel guide.

Inside, the space created by the arched ceilings and sky-high pillars makes you feel small and insignificant. Rays of colored light shine through the circular, rose stained-glass window above the main entrance, adding a dash of brightness to the generally somber interior. Along the recessed walls are dark wooden statues of Jesus and the Virgin Mary touched up with enough gold leaf to make them shine. Some depict him as a baby in her arms, others of her kneeling over his dead body. A few are of just him as an adult on a cross, bleeding from the crown of thorns. The detail of the painted expressions coveys the hope of a new mother and the serene suffering of a martyr with artistic precision and dedication. In front of each display burning candles in red glass cases sit on metal stands. The number of flickering flames varies as if they are votes, with the bloodiest and most gut-wrenching death scene receiving the most light. An open side door reveals yet another dark alley, so you go back to the entrance from which you came.

***

The bright sun outside forces your eyes shut. As they slowly open, the sights and sounds of the square hit your senses. At a metal table glistening in the sun, a group of English tourists sing football chants. Their drunken celebrating bounces off the walls of the surrounding buildings and causes those sitting in the shade of the white umbrellas next door to turn and comment to their companions. A flashing window to a pastry and chocolate shop catches your eye. On the corner is the blue and glass façade of a bar. Flipping through the travel guide to the appropriate section, you read the description. The bar dates back to the eighteenth century and is typical of the time when famous artists like Picasso, Hemingway and Gaudí roamed these very streets. You figure that if it's in the book, it must be a good place to meet people.

The front of the bar is small, but airy and bright with a natural light. It ends at two sets of steps, a short flight which leads down to a tiny room with tables and steep metal ladder leading to an open loft with additional seating. The end of the lunch hour finds only a few stragglers, but the level of their conversation makes the place seem bustling. None of them wear berets or sit at the bar, but most smoke and drink coffee. The polished bottles of spirits on the wooden and mirrored shelves sparkle and a cocktail sounds tempting, but your stomach requests a beer.

There's no sign of a waiter, so you sit down on a cushioned metal stool and pick up a free magazine on the counter near the cash register. On the cover is that strange language, which you now know to be Catalan, next to an upside-down triangle with the mustard and crimson stripes and the black and white donkey from the flag in the newsstand window. Thumbing through the pages, you find photos of a green mountainous landscape of the local countryside conjuring images of knights and dragons in your head. Articles written by men whose photos resemble the bookstore owner, but with more neatly groomed hair, also appear with titles like *Lliure Països Catalans* and *El Problema amb Madrid*. Not all the words are completely indecipherable and *proper* pops up periodically, which you now decide means "next".

Footsteps slap against the linoleum floor and the waiter arrives. Setting down the magazine, you look up to see the girl in the white dress. She wears an unattractive black and white uniform, but she's nevertheless even prettier up close. A jolt of romantic possibility runs through your body at the chance encounter. She offers an ambiguous smile like she remembers you. "*J-es*," she says.

You try to impress her with Spanish. "*Una cerveza.*"

As she takes the biggest jug from the shelf and fills it, she continues to stare at you with her big, brown eyes in a way that makes you think there might be a Hollywood ending to this first day in Barcelona.

"I have a question," you say.

"What?"

"What's the deal with the donkey?"

"It's the national animal of *Catalunya.*"

"Are you Catalan?"

"No, I'm Argentinean. And sorry, but I don't speak much English," she replies, rejecting your overture with the chilly ease of a Manhattan fashion model as breakfast announces its second act.

Senyor Jordi I El Drac

Many centuries ago, on top of the barren and windswept stone peaks of the Pyrenees Mountains, a knight and his squire rode to the click, cluck of their horses' hooves against the rocky eastern ridge. They had been riding to this sound for days on their way to the kingdom of Barcelona, when the wail of a weeping woman cut through the gray air, stopping them in their tracks. So horrifying was the cry that the young squire's face turned white and his normally steady steed, Nano, bucked, neighed, and stopped with a snort and a shake of the head. "What was that, *Senyor* Jordi?" said the boy as he stroked the smooth brown fur of his nervous horse's neck.

"There is only one cry painful and powerful enough to reach us up here my dear, Jaume," replied the old knight. "And that is the cry of a mother who has lost her child."

Lifting the dented visor of his helmet, *Senyor* Jordi squinted his large brown eyes and peered down his long, beak-like nose as he followed the steep slope to where it eased at the trees of the Carlac Forest that stretched north and south like a black band against the brown mountainside. Beyond it were the gray stone and red-tiled roofs of a walled village near a dark lake. He rubbed the white stubble on his thin and worn face, closed his eyes and sighed, "Come on. We must see what we can do."

"Are you sure, sir?"

"Of course, I'm sure. I have not lived the life I've lived to sit around and do nothing when I hear such pain."

"Yes, I know. But something tells me we shouldn't go down there, sir."

"Boy, how many times have I told you that one must fight for what one wants?" He slipped down his visor and took the reins of his white stallion, Anici, signaling an end to the discussion. "Now, come on. We must see what has caused such pain and suffering."

"Yes, sir." The squire gingerly followed his master down a path no wider than the horses' shoulders. The protruding jagged rocks made it seem like they were going mostly sideways as it snaked down the treacherous face of the mountain. Jaume dared not breathe, fearing the slightest noise might literally send him off the cliff which seemed to be constantly on one side. It wasn't until the slope began to flatten and the gravel ground turned to hard dirt that he spoke again. "Sir," he said as they arrived at the first row of barren, twisted black trees of the Carlac Forest.

"What?"

"Should we not rest here for a bit?"

"Jaume, if you wish to go back, by all means, go ahead. You can attack a few windmills in Castilla-La Mancha along the way. I, on the other hand, will be marching forward!"

The squire decided that he had had enough and yanked his horse's reins to turn him around. Nano, however, had other ideas and refused to budge. The boy glared and again tried to steer his steed. And again, Nano refused. Staring into his horse's big brown eyes, the squire realized that the animal's loyalty rested with his master and not him. "Okay, boy, you win," he said kicking the horse's side with spite to spur him along.

As they rode through the desolate wasteland, a thick fog swallowed the barren trees and shriveled bushes. The squire listened for any sound of life – a bird chirping, an insect clicking, a rodent rustling. He heard nothing but the cracks of bones and skulls as they were crushed under their horses' heavy hooves. Whether they were animal, human or both, he did not know, but fear made him shiver.

"Sir!" His shaky voice echoed in the air.

The squire's face again sank in disappointment as he watched his master disappear silently into the fog. Tapping Nano to follow, the young boy cursed his father for sending him with this crazy old knight. All he wanted to do was go home, rest and relax. Life had been easy before and that was how he liked it. Despair had set in when a whiff of burning wood suddenly tickled his nose. He sniffed and lifted his head. A blurry orange speck flashed in the distance. The thought of a fire warmed his frightened and weary soul.

Jaume pointed excitedly. "Do you see the light, sir?"

"What?"

"The light, the light! Do you see it?"

Senyor Jordi's thin lips pursed in concentration and the thousands of lines that etched his face deepened as he stared.

"I don't see anything. Then again, my eyes aren't what they once were," he said turning and smiling at the squire. "Still, I trust you, boy. Let's pay them a visit, shall we?" And for the first time since they had heard the woman's cry atop of the mountain, Jaume didn't complain about his master's decision.

***

The orange speck led to a clearing in the middle of the forest where a small gray building with a red-tiled roof known as a *masia* stood. The shape of a box, made of mortar and uncut small boulders, it was built to keep out the damp cold of winter and the blazing summer sun. But even such a sturdy building could do little to prevent the unease that overcame the young squire at the decay and rot that hung in the air like a foul mist. "Sir," he gagged.

"Almost there, boy." *Senyor* Jordi slowed Anici with a gentle pull of the reins and stopped him with a proud pat on his muscular shoulder. Suppressing a cough, he sat up erect, took off his helmet and tucked it under his right arm. "Ready to see what this is all about?"

"Yes, sir." The squire hopped off Nano and tied him up to a brittle wooden post. Walking over to his master and taking his helmet, he stepped back and watched the old knight push up on the horse's neck. His stick arms shook with effort and his rusted chain mail rattled as his right leg barely cleared Anici's rump. Jaume stepped forward to catch him.

"Back off, boy," *Senyor* Jordi growled as he propped himself up with a hand on each side of the saddle. Taking a deep breath to stop shaking, he relaxed and pushed off, landing with bent knees and a clank. The old knight straightened and faced his squire. "Jaume, I have been doing this by myself since before you were born and will continue doing so. Is that understood?"

"Yes, sir."

"Good." He turned to Anici and tenderly stoked his long, silver mane. "You never doubt me, do you?" he whispered.

The horse replied with a neigh, a spit and a shake of the head.

"Right," *Senyor* Jordi barked strolling to his stallion's side where his trusted sword Ascalon was stored. Grabbing the worn, dyed-green hilt, a *sheeeeeesh* sliced through the air as he unsheathed the long metal blade from its wooden scabbard. The shiny steel caught the light from the house's small windows and a flaming orange ray shone down on the old man standing proudly in a frayed and ragged white tunic with two crossing red lines.

"Let's go," he said, sheathing Ascalon in the leather scabbard on his side as the ray of light faded and the dreary gray sky returned.

"Yes, sir," replied the squire as he followed the knight up a set of crumbling stone steps. His fist pounding on the wooden door brought a scowling woman with long wisps of black hair atop a gaunt white face dotted with red sores.

"Yes," she said in a frail voice that squeaked like rusted hinges.

"I am *Senyor* Jordi. And this is my trusted squire, Jaume."

"Who?"

"*Senyor* Jordi! I was once the emperor's most trusted and valued knight until he asked me to renounce my beliefs and I disobeyed him. He tortured me to the point of death but I was too strong to die!"

"I've never heard of you. We live near Barcelona and are far from Nicemedeia. We have no concern for who is in favor with the emperor and who is not." She paused and pointed to empty pens where healthy, oinking pigs once rolled in their own filth. "As you can see, we are facing a fate worse than any edict he could order."

"Yes, *Senyora*. Please, tell me, what has brought such misery upon you poor people?"

"A dragon."

"A dragon!"

"Yes. It lives in the lake from where we draw our water. At first, it only charged us a sheep and then a pig, but it soon grew bored of our animals' taste." She paused and her listless eyes looked to the ground. "Then it ordered us to bring him our daughters."

"Please tell me you didn't."

"Of course we didn't! We refused, but our answer only angered the beast and it rose from the lake and roared such a roar that all the birds left, never to return."

"Does the dragon breathe fire?" asked the squire, his face pale at the thought.

"No, worse. Its breath carries with it pestilence and death and as it raged through the towns, all our crops and flowers withered and died." She shook her head and her eyes welled with tears. "And when we refused again, it took all our livestock, leaving us only their rotten remains on which to feed."

"That woman's cry we heard?" said the knight.

"That was the queen. The dragon said the king should not be exempt from the suffering of his people and ordered the princess to be the next sacrifice."

"It's got a point," muttered the squire.

"Jaume! No one should have to sacrifice a child to eat and drink," his master replied before turning to the old woman. "Tell us, *Senyora,* where can we find this king?"

She pointed a long bony finger to the black and twisted trees blanketed in a thick fog of the Carlac Forest. "Continue straight down the mountain for about ten minutes and you'll come to a village by the lake. His castle is on the other side."

"Yes, I saw such a village from the mountain's peak. Let's go, boy." *Senyor* Jordi snapped his boots together. "And *Senyora* I promise to rid you people of this dragon."

"Please don't try. I do not want to imagine what he'll do when you fail."

"*Senyora*, one must have faith! Besides, what can be worse than this?"

"Death," she replied slamming the door.

Turning away from the house, the old knight looked at his powerful stallion gnawing on the dirt ground. This was his third Anici. Each one had been the son of the one before and, while they all shared a strength and courage stronger than most men he had known, each had its own distinct personality. The first was stubborn and hard-headed, but the strongest and most courageous. This one carried with it a quiet confidence and strength. "So this is how it is to end - us against the dragon?" he said with a glint in his eye.

"Sir, you don't have to do this," replied the squire.

"You're right. I don't. Then again, I've never had to do most things in life, have I?"

"So why have you done the things you've done, sir?"

"Well, I suppose at first it was to please my father. Like him, I joined the military, but I became a soldier where he was more of a political animal." The knight's armor rattled as he started down the steps with his squire following closely behind.

"And not just any soldier, but one of the emperor's finest, right?"

"I don't know about all that, Jaume. Let's just say a soldier who succeeded to stay alive."

"And then you returned to Nicemedeia."

"I've told you this story before, haven't I?" They stopped at their awaiting horses and *Senyor* Jordi went to Anici's side and returned Ascalon to the wooden scabbard dangling from the saddle. Lifting his boot into the stirrup, he turned to the young boy, "Jaume, give an old man a hand, would you?"

"Yes, sir." The squire eagerly ran over and gave his master a boost up and over the horse that stood so still it could have been a statue.

"Must conserve one's energy," winked the old knight as he settled into the worn saddle and took his batter shield, the crossing red lines on the front.

Jaume looked up through pleading eyes. "Sir, about this dragon... Is it wise? At least let me try."

"That is very brave of you boy. But you are not ready, and this is my battle."

"Yes, sir. But, a dragon?"

"Yes, I know what we're facing." He patted Anici's shoulders and took the reins. "Now, no more talk. Mount up and let's go. There is a princess to save!" he shouted, trusting his arm in the air. His powerful stallion lifted up its front legs and kicked in excitement at the news. The squire's nervous stomach, meanwhile, knotted in a familiar disappointment as he slunk towards his snorting horse.

***

The dense fog soon began to thin, revealing the few mangled tree stumps at the forest's edge and the start of a gradual dirt slope. The brown wall of the village was not too far off in the distance. Looking at his master sitting on his white horse with his head up and his back straight, the squire remembered the day his father brought the beaten and bloodied man to their home.

As the story went, after fighting in the emperor's many wars for twenty years, *Senyor* Jordi returned to Nicemedeia a changed man. But instead of retiring into politics like most decorated soldiers, he chose to speak out against the emperor and his edicts and give away all his wealth in the process. The squire once asked his father, "Why?" and his old man responded, "Living through war changes a person."

His father was the only one who offered this rational. Most subscribed to the theories that *Senyor* Jordi had converted to some barbaric, foreign religion and eventually even his old friend the emperor turned on him, ordering him to be lashed on a wheel of swords outside the city's walls. When Jaume asked the knight the reason behind his change, he replied, "Everyone can change. It's just a matter of choosing to or choosing not to, and I chose to," and switched the topic.

***

"Jaume, look at this place." *Senyor* Jordi's gravelly voice stopped the squire from thinking about the past as the full horror of the village through which they now rode came down like a fiery sermon. People pushing wheelbarrows stacked with dead bodies dumped their morbid contents against the gray stone of the buildings like trash. In the main square starving men, women and children gathered and begged for food from the chubby priest standing outside the temple's walls. For the first time in his young life, Jaume understood desperation.

"Now, do you see why we must try and do something," said the knight.

"It is truly horrible, sir. But why us? Can't someone else do it?"

"Why not us?"

"Because we can't!"

"Perhaps not, if we try. But for sure, if we don't."

"But *Senyor* Jordi, you will die."

"And so will you one day, Jaume. How you can look around and feel all this misery and destruction and not be moved to do something other than complain is beyond me." He gently spurred his nervous, spitting horse. "But, I – for one – cannot, and will not, sit idly by."

"But to battle with a dragon, sir? Is there not something else we can do?"

"I hope so. I haven't been in combat in ten years."

A man's desperate pleas cut their conversation short. *Senyor* Jordi grabbed his wooden shield, banged on it, and slid down his dented visor.

"The time is upon us," he said kicking Anici from a trot into a canter.

Galloping with the wind smacking against his face and the rapid clicks and clucks of Nano's hooves hitting the cobble-stone streets echoing in his head, the young squire forgot where they were heading. He rode so fast with all his concentration focused on staying on his horse that the world ceased to exist as he flew out of the back gate of the walled village. Nano hit the ground in perfect stride and Jaume imagined a different present where he rode towards his neighbor's daughter, the beautiful Elisenda, who awaited him with open arms. The sight of the round lake with water so black and still that it looked like tar, soon brought back his fear of the future. The squire pulled on the reins to slow down and watched his master approach a rag-tag group of villagers on the banks.

"What's going on here?" beckoned *Senyor* Jordi.

"They want to sacrifice my daughter," cried a voice.

"It's the only way! It's the only way!" screamed the group as a fat man with a thick brown beard and a gold embroidered velvet tunic pushed his way through to the front.

His lips quivering as he spoke, he said, "I am the king."

"Bring me your daughter," commanded *Senyor* Jordi and the villagers parted to reveal a woman chained to a stake by the lake's rocky bank. A stunning beauty with long golden locks and sparkling hazel eyes, the pearl and lace girdle of the wedding dress she wore boosted her ample bosom and hugged her round curves. *Senyor* Jordi, noticing his squire's slack jaw, pulled alongside and said, "You'd fight a dragon for that, wouldn't you, boy?"

Jaume turned red and offered no reply.

The knight returned his gaze to the princess and lifted up his visor. "What's this I hear about you being sacrificed?"

Her trembling voice tried to be firm. "Please, I understand you are a knight and it is your nature to be chivalrous and valiant, but leave us be."

"I don't understand."

"The dragon promised to return the lake and our land if my father sacrificed me."

"That is nonsense. There will be no more death!"

A hiss erupted from the depths of the lake that shook the ground. Rising up, it grew louder and crashed through the black surface with a deafening splash, sending water cascading down like a rain of arrows. In the gray sky, a red scaled beast with the black wings of a bat and the head of a snake stretched its arms and legs that were nothing but loosely connected bones. It looked down and roared.

The villagers had little desire to face its wrath again and fled while the king hid behind a large rock, leaving only the chained princess, the knight and his squire in its dark shadow. "This girl is not to be sacrificed and you are to give the lake back to the village," *Senyor* Jordi shouted as he closed his visor and drew his sword.

Ascalon glistened and the beast hissed. This time it was more like a laugh than a roar of anger. Flapping its wings to thunderous claps, it soared higher into the air where it became just a dot in the sky. Suddenly it dove down like a spear launched from a catapult with an ear-piercing squeal that cracked the stone houses of the village. "Hold," ordered the knight with his shield up and his sword steady on his hip, his trembling squire at his side.

The dragon spread its wings to slow its descent. Like the bat from whose form they took, they moved and fluttered in every direction and angle, giving them a hypnotic quality that held the knight and his squire in a trance. Growing closer, the beast cast an ever darkening shadow over them as it stretched a skeletal arm across its chest and unleashed a back hand smack. The blow rattled Jaume's helmet and sent him crashing to the ground. Pain numbed his muscles and he could only watch as the laughing dragon flew higher and higher, disappearing from sight. Again, it screamed down. The knight did not hold this time, but turned and spurred Anici into a desperate sprint that left a cloud of dust as he raced towards the cover of the forest.

Waiting to feel the dragon's icy breath on his neck, *Senyor* Jordi said a prayer for courage and strength and yanked the reins of his galloping horse, taking a hard right. The beast furiously flailed its wings in futile attempt to stop its forward momentum. Anici's hooves slid and skidded, its legs almost buckling from the sharpness of a turn that barely evaded the onrushing dragon as it crashed into the trees, flipping over, landing on its back.

"You're breath is really quite rank," teased *Senyor* Jordi, as he steadied his proud, neighing horse.

The dragon rolled onto its belly and began to rise. Slowly spreading its massive wings like a black cape, the towering beast stood on its hind legs and pointed at the knight daring him to make his next move.

Senyor Jordi traced the red lines that crossed his tunic, cocked the mighty Ascalon back, and charged. The horse's pounding hooves sounded like the drums of war and the dragon hissed in excitement as it flung its head back to strike. Leaping high in the air, Anici hurtled itself towards the attacking beast, passing just under its clamping jaws. *Senyor* Jordi sensed the moment to deal the victorious blow, lunged and thrust the long blade deep into the red scales of dragon's neck, the surrounding trees exploding from a deafening scream as man, beast and horse collided.

***

The pain and ringing in Jaume's head had dulled to the point where the young squire contemplated getting up. Dazed like he had just lost a joust, he rolled onto his stomach, pushed up onto his knees, and staggered to his feet. Looking around, he swayed and saw blurry doubles of a thin man walking towards him with his visor up and a shining smile across his face. "*Senyor* Jordi, you're alive!" cried the squire who knew at that moment that he would never doubt or question his master again.

"Of course, boy. I'm not going to lose to a reptile, no matter how big it is." Tapping his head to re-enforce the lesson, he said, "The number one rule of a soldier, pick one's battles wisely. Dragons are a predictable lot. Fly up, swoop down and bite."

"Is it dead?"

"No. In fact, dust yourself off and come with me. I want to show you something. Nano's waiting for you." He brought the young boy in close and hugged him like a son as they strolled towards the now blue lake's rocky edge.

***

Where the dragon's crimson had been spilled the horses munched on the first shoots of green grass that the land had seen in years. Listing to the rustle of a breeze, the squire swore he heard the faint chirp of a bird as he watched an elated princess run up to *Senyor* Jordi and kiss him over and over again. "I can't thank you enough," she said.

His wrinkled white face blushed red. "That's alright. I'm a knight. I had to do something."

"And you are the bravest one at that!"

"According to my squire - a stupid one. Right, Jaume?"

"Hum," he coughed. "I've never called you stupid."

"So," said the king. "What do we do with the dragon?" He spoke deeply and forcefully, conveying a restored sense of power and authority.

"Princess," said the knight. "Would you do an old man a favor and take off your girdle?"

"You want me to do what?"

"Please, I want to show you something." *Senyor* Jordi walked to the young girl's back and clumsily undid the first knot of string. Watching them, the squire became entranced by her beauty and a dribble of drool formed in the corner of his mouth. The king's firm hand on his shoulder reminded him that he was not alone.

"You see." *Senyor* Jordi slipped the girdle over the head and around the neck of a beast which no longer seemed so big and menacing, but more like an animal at the emperor's zoo, "Completely meek and compliant."

"Are we supposed to keep it as a pet?" asked the king.

"No, follow me," replied the knight as he led the defeated dragon up the smooth slope by a long rope with the king, princess and squire at his side. Cries of horror and the slam of doors greeted them at the brown wall of the village. "Be not afraid people, for the beast has been vanquished."

The crack of doors and windows opening was followed by the buzz of conversation as the skeletal villagers slowly trickled out from behind the wall to see if the crazy old knight was right. "Why isn't it dead? Why isn't it dead?" they demanded to know.

"I will slay it on one condition."

"What? What? What?"

"That you renounce the life you had before the dragon," he replied. "A life where a few individuals are strong, but the village is weak; a life where a dragon can come, take your lake and make you sacrifice your own children just to live on the rotten remains of all that you once had. For if you don't do this, this will not be the last dragon to visit your land!"

Senyor Jordi's speech had the king squirming and the people chanting, "We swear! We swear! We swear!"

He raised the sparkling Ascalon into the sky one last time. As it sliced through the gray air, it caught a faint ray of the sun and flashed like an exploding star before coming down across the dragon's neck to a joyous cheer from the crowd.

"A blood thirsty lot," muttered Jaume.

His comment did not go unnoticed and the princess's hazel eyes glared to show that she was not amused.

"Thank you, thank you," said the king looking twenty years younger. "You are a true saint! My brother is the Count of Barcelona and I will tell him to erect buildings and anoint a holiday in your honor!"

31

"Please don't. Just try to heed my words. As you can see, I am an old man who won't be around to save you the next time." He stroked Anici's shoulders and turned to Jaume. "Come on, boy. Let's go."

"Where to now, sir?"

"Why don't we pay our old friend Don Quixote a visit and see how many dragons he's slain, shall we?" the knight replied as he and his squire rode towards a forest of budding flowers and singing birds to the muffled click, cluck of their horses' hooves against the soft, grassy ground.

A Book for a Rose

A blaring alarm clock woke Johnny up to a painful hangover from drinking to the end of a romantic dream. The time: 7:00 a.m. He hit the snooze button and buried his head in the pillow. The previous night had been spent trying to forget Elena's news over multiple beers with his friends at a bar, but the sting of knowing whatever slight chance there was between them was finished, still burned. An extra hour or two or three of rest was what his throbbing head really needed. She would take a bit longer. He debated calling work and canceling his first business English class due to eating some bad Kebab, but his grandmother's favorite expression, "There's no rest for the wicked," spoken in her stern Midwestern accent played in his head as a reminder of his responsibilities. He rolled out of bed and turned off the alarm before the second snooze sounded.

His bedroom was just off a white-walled living room. About the size of a storage closet, it had a small window that looked onto the gray stone of the adjoining building, a two-seater wooden couch with a straight-backed chair across from it and a television that was smaller than a laptop. He thought about the last time he went to the states and saw his old friends. They were all in their early-to-mid thirties. Those who could afford it had moved on to the house buying stage of their lives and taken out thirty-year mortgages on two-or-three-bedroom homes with spacious living rooms, using the

33

equity to furnish them lavishly. Even those who still rented had a decent apartment with a comfortable living space that sat more than three. And, it seemed, everyone had a flat-screen, high-definition television.

The living room led to a narrow corridor that ended at another bedroom, where his Dutch flat mate lived and the entrance to the flat. Passing a closed door on his right, he heard the faint snoring of his other flat mate, Germano. Half-Portuguese and half-African, he had moved in a year ago after getting his business degree at an English university and now he worked at a banking call center for just over a thousand Euros a month - the bare minimum needed to live in Barcelona.

Next was a blue tiled bathroom, so small, it was literally built for one person and one person only. Taking off his boxer shorts, he stepped over the toilet bowl and entered a shower barely wider than his hips. The hot water spraying against his face eased the tension in his head and he thought of the first time he met Elena as he lathered up and scrubbed the smell of last night's tobacco from his body.

***

Her regular teacher had still been in Australia, so Johnny substituted for the first class after Christmas break. He expected her to be like most of his female students - in their late forties, easy to talk to with a decent level of English, but with a hard Spanish accent of hacks for 'H' and 'Y' and for 'J' an abrupt tone, but he had been pleasantly surprised to discover otherwise.

Just a year older than him and already the H.R. Director of a German multinational, Elena was the quintessential Spanish beauty with long, silky black hair and large, almost black, eyes. She spoke English with the charming intonation of a European actress in a

Hollywood production and for eighty-five minutes, it seemed as if the dream he'd had when he was eight of coming to Spain and meeting a dark-haired beauty was about to be realized. The only thing left to complete the vision was the house on the beach, the dog and her in a white dress. The revelation of a husband fifteen years her senior who had left his wife and two kids to be with her, and whose first present to her was thoroughbred horse, brought the romantic possibility to a screeching stop and the class to an end. Walking out the building, Johnny was ready to file her image away for those lonely nights at home when his boss called. Elena had requested him as her permanent teacher and, from that point on, they met twice a week, every week and she never missed a class.

***

Following the shower, Johnny quickly dressed in wrinkled slacks and a button-down shirt, grabbed his backpack by the door and walked out of the flat. The slippery stone steps varied just ever so slightly in height and width making each step down a question of recalibrating basic motor skills. On the second floor, old widow Teresa sat on a stool by her open door and cut out newspaper articles. "*Hola cariño.* Are you going to work?" she asked in a creaky voice as she smiled and put down the scissors.

"*Bon dia*, Teresa. Yes, and I'm running late as usual." He spoke to her mostly in Spanish with some Catalan thrown in. Looking at the wall, he saw it was plastered with highlighted columns detailing the corruption at the municipal and regional offices and the proposed cuts in social services.

"You look a little sad?" She slowly stood up from the stood and took his hand.

He smiled politely at her cold touch. "I'm okay."

"Do you know what today is?"

"No, what?"

"*Sant Jordi.*"

"That's right! I'd forgotten. *Bon Sant Jordi*, Teresa."

Footsteps coming down from the floors above interrupted the conversation and Johnny slowly freed his hand from Teresa's grip as Paco, the thirty-five year man who lived with his mother in the apartment across the hall, sprinted down the stairs. "*Adéu,*" he blurted.

Teresa watched the man descend and disappear down the next flight of steps. "He's a strange and rude boy," she said looking at Johnny through thick glasses for confirmation.

"I'm sure he's just in a rush." He glanced down the set of steps. "Alright, Teresa, I gotta go."

"Wait," she snapped going into her dark and moldy apartment and coming out with a book. "As is the tradition today." She gave him a used paperback written in Catalan about Barcelona's most famous architect, Antoni Gaudí, and his benefactor, Eusebi Güell.

"*Moltes gràcies,*" Johnny said in thanks, bending down and kissing her cheek. "I owe you a rose now." He looked at his watch. The time was 8:20. Class started in ten minutes.

***

The first class of the day was a one-to-one with the financial director of the same German multinational where Elena worked. The offices were in the tall copper building on Carrer Tarragona near Plaça Espanya and it was a fifteen minute stroll from the flat if he took it slow. That day he hoisted his heavy backpack over both shoulders and marched with long strides and pumping arms, arriving at the sliding glass doors in eight minutes.

Panting and hot from the near run, he flapped his button down shirt to cool off before he went in. His cell phone rang. "*Si*."

"*Hola, Yonni*. It's Monica," she said in English.

"Hey, Monica."

"Sorry for the late notice. There's a note on my desk saying Manel can't attend class this morning."

A little advance warning would've been nice, Johnny thought, but either way he got paid and with his next lesson not until the early afternoon, he couldn't complain too much. "Um, okay. No problem. Tell him to call me the next time he cancels, though."

"You know how he is. Hopefully see you next week." The line went dead and he made a u-turn and walked down a short set of steps. On his way home, he thought about Elena.

***

Most of their classes were spent at the bar by her office drinking coffee and talking about each other's lives and dreams. Every time they saw each other, they communicated with an ease and honesty that reminded him of his friends back home. When she told Johnny about her goal of leaving the corporate world and becoming an independent business coach, he offered her encouragement and support, citing his move to Barcelona to concentrate on writing as an example of chasing an ambition. When she described her husband, estranged from his siblings and antisocial with everyone but her, he said nothing, although his clenched expression did little to disguise his dislike for a man who he did not believe to be worthy.

Sometimes, after her husband was brought up, Johnny steered the topic to the women he dated. It always produced a flash of jealousy in what were normally soulful and serene eyes followed by a comment that these girls weren't good enough for him. And over the months, the seed of hope was planted that maybe, perhaps, his romantic dream had not come to an end just yet. When the topic of sex started popping up more and more during their conversations, it grew into a real possibility. Yesterday's news dug up the chance of anything romantic between them and ran over it with a car.

***

The time was 8:50 a.m. by the time Johnny got back to his room. The twenty minute march to and from Plaça Espanya had his blood rushing and his heart pumping. He felt little desire to sleep. Sitting down at his desk and turning on up his laptop, he looked out the window to the antennas on the tops of the buildings and an overcast sky. This spring has been unusually wet, he thought before realizing he thought the same thing every year. Still, as he rubbed the temples of his tender head, he wondered if it would be the first Saint George's day in history that the sun didn't shine.

The chime of his computer booting up brought his attention to his laptop's screen and he double-clicked the browser icon to log onto the net. His homepage loaded to an inbox full of bold new messages. Many were job postings from numerous employment websites he had registered with last week. They were positions in London with decent salaries working in his pre-Spain profession as an account manager for a software company. A few had a personal note from a recruiter mentioning he'd have a better chance if he moved to England. Mixed in with these were rejection letters from agents regarding his latest novel. Finally, there was also note from Elena wondering if he would be interested in a position that recently opened up at her company. He didn't feel like answering any of his messages and logged out of his inbox.

He wasted a good hour surfing the Internet, reading about his favorite sports teams and visiting pages like Facebook to see what his friends and family in the states were doing. Some were married and a couple had children. Others were still swinging single or divorced. A few maintained a relationship out of comfort and convenience. Those who came from good family stock and could afford a decent university education had settled into professional careers, began a small business, or became public school teachers. Those who didn't worked in sales, real-estate or retail. Everyone commented on how busy they were.

He checked his bank account. The company he worked for was basically an agency offering English courses to businesses and individuals. He received an above-average hourly salary for every class that fell on a work day, regardless if the students came or not as stated in the contact, resulting in some days getting paid to do nothing. Johnny's boss told him to tell anyone who complained to think of it as a gym membership. But it didn't offer any benefits in the way of vacation or sick days, nor did it pay on any of the fourteen public holidays, during the two month summer break, or the three-weeks at Christmas.

This meant from January through March, the only months when there were no *fiestas*, he had to work hard and save. Easter signaled the start of spring, after which point every month had at least one day off. July and August followed and the only work available then was in summer camps with hundreds of screaming, pampered kids or week-long intensive classes with adults that took place in a remote house in the mountains. There were three students and three teachers for five days and nights and no way of escaping for a quiet moment until you went to sleep. Classes started again at the middle of September which meant Christmas and the week-long holiday at the beginning of December were just around the corner.

That said, compared to the litany of other jobs he had done, ranging from cold-caller for a stock broker to restaurant bartender to tech support rep, it wasn't that bad. He didn't work in an office, most of his students were easy to teach and twenty hours a week was a full load, meaning he could spend his free time writing and working on his craft. Coming to the end of the partying stage of his life, he no longer felt that insatiable itch to go out every night like he did in the past, fearing what he'd miss if he didn't. With his back free of that mad, fun-loving monkey, he was able to weather the peaks and valleys of the job well enough to enjoy the craziness of Barcelona on the weekends and travel Europe during his long vacations. And best of all, he didn't need of a credit card to survive.

His blood no longer rushing, his heart slowed. Drowsiness arrived like a slowly creeping fog rolling in from the sea, blanking his brain with the desire to sleep as his eyes grew heavy. His head still needed an hour or two more of rest to stop hurting. Switching off the computer and swiveling his seat around, he faced his double-bed two feet away and jumped. The frame and mattress creaked as he crawled under the comforter, hugged a pillow and closed his eyes.

**

A wheezing drill penetrated his deep sleep and promptly stopped once Johnny was awake. Prying open his eyes to a groggy, post-nap headache, he heard the muffled sound of the TV on the other side of the wall and got out of bed to see who it was. He found Germano laying on the couch with pillows against the wooden arms in an attempt to make it comfortable. "Hey dude," his flat mate said.

They had originally agreed to speak in Spanish, but with Germano near fluent and Johnny merely conversational, they communicated in English in which they were basically equals. Johnny rubbed his eyes and yawned, "Hey, man. What's up?"

"Not much, just watching the local news. I guess a guy got five years for attacking a civil servant."

"No shit." Johnny looked at the small TV and saw a picture of an unassuming man on the small screen. "What you doing home?"

"My work contract ended last week and I decided not to renew it."

"You gonna look for another job?"

"No, I'm gonna use my severance and unemployment benefits to travel Spain and then go back to the U.K. and study a masters."

"You're not staying here?"

"Barcelona's a great city and I've had so much fun, but there's not much work with good pay, you know?"

"But it rains all the time in England." Johnny had grown fond of his young flat mate and hoped to discourage the move despite halfheartedly contemplating it himself.

"Yeah, I know. But it hasn't stopped raining here for the last two months."

Johnny laughed in agreement as he sat down on the chair and looked at his friend. "But summer will be here soon. Why don't you teach? Your English is excellent. The pay is decent and not too many hours. I can get you a job."

"It's not really my thing. I was thinking of getting into import-export with my family from Africa."

Johnny no longer tried to change people's minds. He had seen too many friends come and go such was the transient nature of the city. "Yeah, I can understand that. When you leaving?"

"The end of the month." Germano sat up, "Do you think you'll ever go back to the states?"

"When I can buy a house in Malibu and have a driver."

Germano laughed at the chances of that happening, "Seriously?"

"I don't know. I've got this gap on my resume now, stacks of unpaid credit card bills and I really, really hate driving." Johnny looked to the round clock on the wall. The time was 12:20. He jumped up and ran to his room. "Shit, I'm running late again."

***

His next class was in the Maria Cristina district of Barcelona. Located at a building famous for the plants that hung from its windows, it was a major Spanish media company that owned a TV station, three newspapers and published the majority of books in Spain and South America. Walking into the windowless meeting room, Johnny took a seat at a round table with six chairs. Nobody had arrived yet, so he took out a book and started reading.

"Hi *Yonni*," said a male voice fifteen pages later.

"Hey Enric." Johnny put his book in the bag and looked at the clock on his mobile to see it was already ten minutes into class.

"Sorry I'm late. I needed to eat something quickly," his student explained taking the seat with the best view of the free standing white board.

"No problem. How's everything?"

"Good. My boss said he'd give me a sabbatical if I found an internship with a newspaper in England or the states."

"That's great. Let me know if I can help with applications or anything."

"Hi Johnny." It was two female voices.

"Hey, Nuria. Hey, Montse."

"Sorry we're late," they said in unison as they sat two seats away from Enric.

"No problem." He stood up and walked to the white board. "How's everyone today?"

"Great! I went out on a date!" Nuria's plump cheeks turned pink with excitement.

"That's fantastic. And what about you, Montse?"

She finished checking her face in the compact and looked up. "It was fun. Carlos and I went to *Danzatoria* and partied until six."

"I've been there. It's a bit posh, isn't it?"

"He gets free passes."

"I see."

Nuria took out a small notebook. "No grammar or listenings today, right? They're so boring! And work's been really hard lately."

"No, I thought we'd do conversation and correction." Johnny took out a marker and readied to teach. "With it being *Sant Jordi*, the topic is books." He wrote a series of ten questions mixing the tenses, vocabulary and grammar points he remembered teaching so far that year and used the answers to generate a discussion. It was the same class he did every April 23rd. The three students, who all had advance levels, managed to get

43

through the hour and fifteen minutes with Johnny needing to correct them only once, making his job seem pointless and too easy sometimes.

***

After working for an hour and a half and with his next class not until late afternoon, Johnny had time to kill but didn't feel like heading home. Two fellow teachers stood outside the building's exit, smoking and chatting. "Hey Brad," he said to the taller and lankier of the two.

"Hey man." A fellow U.S. citizen, Brad had settled in Spain after impregnating a Catalan girl during a summer working at a bar on Ibiza and spoke with a monotone droll of a man who went through the motions of life. "I haven't seen you around in a while. How's things?"

"Went out a bit hard last night."

"Any reason?"

"Usual shit – life, women." He turned to the shorter teacher. "How's everything, Tim?"

"'ello, mate," he said in the Queen's English. "I wanted to do a *bah* and conversation class again, because, quite frankly, the Spanish need to speak and listen to English more." Taking a long drag of a cigarette, his prison vocabulary came out as he went on a tirade. "But as always is the fucking case, that cunt Ester complained. She wanted to study bloody, fucking grammar again."

"Dude. Why not just do grammar the first half of class and convo the second?"

"Because she wants to know the difference between 'can' and 'to be able to' when she can't even use the fucking simple past correctly."

"I don't even know the difference between them," said Brad, putting out his cigarette in an ashtray by the building's door.

"Hell, I didn't even know what the 'simple past' was until I became a teacher here," added Johnny flicking the butt of his smoke onto the pavement. "What you guys up to now?"

Brad took his backpack and slung it over his shoulders, "Gonna grab lunch. Wanna join?"

"Sure."

They walked away from the building towards a main street under a sky that had lightened to an almost elephant gray, hinting at the possibility of a break in the spring gloom. Large gypsy women sitting at folding tables with plastic buckets of flowers manned the intersections of the cross streets. Their long hair pulled back into a pony-tails, they waved individually wrapped roses at passers-by and reminded them not to forget their mother. Looking around at the scene, Johnny said, "What book did your wife get you, Brad?"

"Something called *The Secret*."

Tim's round face twisted in disgust. "That new-age bollocks!"

"Yeah. She says my perception of life is too negative and that's why I'm so unhappy," Brad deadpanned as they came to the large window of a restaurant. "It has nothing to do with the fact that I don't love her and I hate Spain, but I don't want to leave my kid."

"Jesus, dude." Johnny didn't know what else to say to a man in such dire straits as he looked inside a restaurant for a place to sit. It was buzzing and full of business men and women in conservative suits eating, drinking coffee and smoking. The slight chance of rain meant that the patio was empty. "Other than the wife and not liking Spain, how's life otherwise?" he said hoping for a little lighter topic as they sat down outside to eat.

"Alright. I really need to find something else to do. I'm just not a teacher, you know?"

"Yeah. We say the same thing every time we see each other. I've been looking for work in the London recently."

Tim sat up in a rage. "Why on earth would you fucking want to go there, mate? It's bloody, fucking miserable. That's why we Brits all come here."

"Teaching's like restaurant work with better hours. But it offers the same nowhere future, you know?"

"Your Spanish is good enough. Why not work for a company here?

"Dude, after teaching the Spanish, I can't work for them. All they like to do is have three-hour meetings."

Brad's glum face showed emotion for the first time and he laughed. "What about your writing?"

"I got a lot of hits of the query letter and synopsis. A few agents asked for the complete manuscript. I haven't heard anything back, though."

Tim looked into the restaurant and waved for the waiter. "It's not an easy thing, mate."

"Yeah, I know. I just don't think if I have it in me to write another novel. It's such a massive undertaking with no sure payoff at the end. And if I can't be a writer, I feel this need to find a career in something that impresses people."

Brad nodded in agreement and replied, "That's the American in us," as the waiter came to the table.

On the window was a chalkboard with the day's set menu. For a first dish, the options were one of three choices: macaroni in a Bolognese sauce, a Spanish salad with all the usual suspects (lettuce, tomato, onion, etc.) and canned tuna, or a plate of paella. For seconds, there was roasted chicken with fries, a grilled Catalan sausage with peas or a baked hake with a salad. A drink and dessert were also included. The total price was ten Euros. They ordered their meals and continued talking.

Being expats gave them a common bond which allowed them to speak freely and openly as if good friends, despite coming from such different backgrounds and even though they only saw each other a few times a year. None of them were teachers by profession, their jobs simply a result of speaking the English language, so they discussed different ways to explain the various tenses and keep students interested, because they hadn't a clue but wanted to do their jobs well. They shared in the frustrations and joys that came with living in this strange land before changing the subject to the state of their lives. Tim was happy and content, Brad miserable and Johnny somewhere in-between. He didn't tell them about Elena, not feeling that close to them, but he did offer a story from last weekend involving throwing firecrackers off a friend's balcony. Tim laughed and Brad wished he were single. Switching from the present to the past at times, their tone changed from friendly to whimsical as they remembered their former lives and plans, recalling family and friends with a bittersweet longing of a world that no longer existed. And when the check came, they paid and went their separate ways with no set date to meet again - such was the nature of many expat friendships in the city.

***

While sitting on a relatively empty metro, Johnny read a blurb in the free newspaper about a vigilante who had gone after the muggers of *El Raval* and *Barrio Gotico*. A victim of the infamous pickpockets of Barcelona, he could sympathize with the desire for vengeance. His phone rang and he set down the paper.

"*Hola* Johnny." It was Elena.

Hearing her soft voice made the lingering dull pain in his head go away and replaced it with the sting of remorse.

"Hey. Sorry I haven't gotten back to you yet. I've been a bit busy."

"That's okay. Would you like to meet for a coffee today? I'm leaving work now to walk around the city-center for a little bit."

"I'd love to, but I gotta plan for the next class."

"It's *Sant Jordi*! I'm sure they'll cancel." She paused for a split second pause. "It'll only be a few minutes. I have something for you."

"You didn't have to get me anything."

"I wanted to. I'd like to see you."

"Okay." He got off the metro at the next stop, walked up and down a set of stairs and went to the platform for the other direction. The clock hanging from the ceiling said, *Proper tren 2:09*.

***

They agreed to meet at the bottom of Rambla Catalunya near Plaça Catalunya. Not as famous as Las Ramblas of the Gothic quarter, it was Johnny's favorite street in Barcelona. Smaller and more intimate than most of the other *ramblas* found throughout the city, the organic forms of the late nineteen century buildings and the lush trees made the promenade feel more like a walk through a forest than the middle of an urban center. The only thing more magnificent was the beautiful Elena waiting by a row of scooters on the corner. "*Hola*, Johnny," she said as they kissed each other's cheeks.

Her fresh fragrance made him think of being alone with her in a mountain cabin on a week-long intensive. "*Hola*, Elena."

"Happy *Sant Jordi*."

He looked at the small foothills bordering Barcelona to the west and focused on the stone church with a massive statue of Christ and an amusement park atop Tibidabo Mountain. The clouds beyond it broke and a dash of the blue sky made its first appearance in the horizon. He didn't feel too sunny.

"*Bon Sant Jordi*."

The Catalan made her smile and him want to learn more. "I got a present for you," she said handing him a white paper bag.

Reaching in, he pulled out a paperback with the title: *My Christina and Other Stories* by Mercè Rodoreda. He checked out the back. "It's in English."

"I ordered it for you. She was a famous Catalan writer during the modernist times."

"Thank you, Elena." He gave her a kiss on the cheek. "I owe you a rose now."

She took his arm and put her head on his shoulder. "Don't worry about it. Let's walk for a bit."

***

Sant Jordi wasn't a public holiday, but judging by the thousands of people on the festive streets, it seemed to be. Celebrated only in *Catalunya* and ignored in the rest of Spain, it was a source of tremendous regional pride. The five vertical crimson and mustard stripes of the Catalan nation were everywhere from the hanging flags of the overlooking balconies to the backs of the otherwise clear cellophane that wrapped the roses to the cloths draping the long tables from which stacks of books were sold.

The throngs of people lazily strolling and stopping at the temporary white tents along the street caused Johnny's body temperature to rise. "How's everything going?" he asked trying to suppress the growing anxiety that crowded situations brought.

"Okay. Sergi's taking his sons sailing this weekend if the weather's good." She lifted her head off his shoulder and studied him. Her soulful stare was like a cool breeze, easing the rising tension by making everyone around him disappear. "How are you? You look a bit sad."

"Same ol', same ol'. In a rut."

"In a what?"

Sometimes Johnny forgot she wasn't fluent in English and he rephrased the sentence, "I just don't know what to do anymore."

"What about the position in my company? We could work together."

He looked into an unblinking and sincere face. "That's very kind, Elena. But, I don't think I'm cut out for office work anymore. The years living here have made me a bit lazy."

She laughed and he didn't feel like a slacker. "What is it you'd like to do then?"

"Write."

"You'd like to be the next Dan Brown?"

"I'd be happy with a hundredth of his success." Thinking about what he'd truly like to accomplish, he looked at the thousands of people who bought books and said, "It'd just be nice to earn a decent living doing the only thing I enjoy, you know?"

She smiled and he believed it to be possible. "You're such a brave man coming here and chasing a dream. It's a shame you can't meet a woman to support you." She gently stroked his cheek and looked tenderly into his eyes, "If only I were single, that's what I'd do."

Johnny teared at such a beautiful thought. He snickered at the absurdity of knowing it was never going to happen.

Elena's soft lips turned up into a sly grin. "Our contract with your company ends this month. I'll tell them we're going in a different direction and hire you as the in-house teacher. I'll pay you what we pay them. I imagine it'll double your salary so you can work less."

All of Johnny's muscles went limp and his jaw dropped at the unexpected offer. "Wow, I don't know what to say."

"Don't say anything. Just use the free time to write." She smiled and his spirits lifted at the elation at finding a person who believed in him.

"And when I publish something, you'll be the first person I thank." He imagined the glorious day and beamed.

"That would be very nice." Elena's round eyes sparkled like black pearls. He recognized the look. It was one he had seen only a few times in his life. Some called it carnal attraction, but he preferred to think of it as the possibility of achieving a shared romantic dream, if even for an instant. The moment lasted a few seconds, but it was enough to have a fleeting glimpse of an alternate future with her in a white dress and a dog on the beach. Her eyes clouded and dulled with the reality of the situation. "I told my boss about my pregnancy."

Johnny's face went stoic in an attempt to mask the sting that those words still brought. Taking a deep breath, he swallowed the bitter disappointment and stomached it like he did every time a rejection letter arrived in his inbox. It tasted like curdled milk left out in the hot sun for a week.

"How'd he take it?"

"He was a bit angry because Carla has just got back from maternity leave and Sonia only got back from Russia with her little boy last December."

"It's a regular baby boom at the office," he chuckled.

"I suppose. We were hoping to wait until next year, but you can't plan these things."

"You'll make a great mother, Elena."

"I hope so, *cariño*. I never thought I wanted kids until recently." She looked at her dangling gold watch, "I'd better go. I have a meeting at five and I still need to get Sergi's book." She held his arm and gave a soft peck on each cheek. "We'll see each other next week."

"Okay." Johnny watched her slink down the street and disappear into the mass of people buying books and roses. The faint romantic dream that they'd somehow be together was over like his life in the states leaving with it the same bittersweet aftertaste of, "What if?" But it wasn't as strong as this morning and in its place was a feeling similar to when he was fourteen and had to read *Great Expectations* for his English class. The book had caused him to spend the rest of his life wondering what it would be like to have a benefactor. Now, he had one, kind of. At least she's better looking than Miss Havisham, he thought.

Determination filled his body like the first hit of a drug. He stood tall and ready to conquer the world. He was going to repay her faith in him the only way he knew how - by writing. Looking to the sky for inspiration, he followed the gray clouds being pushed by an easterly breeze towards the sea. They moved like a slowly lifting curtain unveiling a celestial blue sky fit for the ceiling of a cathedral. The statuesque buildings of Rambla Catalunya sparkled and came alive in the yellow sunlight and the smell of fresh flowers and wet leaves tickled his nose. He decided whatever story he wrote needed to be set in Barcelona – the most beautiful and original city in the world and a place rich in inspiration.

***

Elena was right. His students canceled their class on account of wanting to enjoy the late afternoon sun, walking around, buying books and flowers. On the way to his flat, Johnny stopped to get a rose for old widow Teresa. A gypsy woman with penetrating black eyes showed him the choices. There was the traditional red, in addition to some blue, white, and yellow. The sad state of the loose petals revealed them to be of a poor quality, but the woman's dark stare made him fearful of a hex if he didn't buy one so he did.

He was tired from the all the walking by the time he got to his building. Taking out a large brass key, he sighed. He lived on the fourth floor, which due to the *entresuelo* and *planta prinicpal*, was really five and a half flights up. And despite climbing the stairs literally thousands of time in his three years there, he still hadn't gotten used to it. To remedy the situation, he had put up an ad on Loquo looking for a new place to live last week and received a response for a great exterior room in Plaça Urquinaona with a view of the plaça. The job offer from Elena meant he could afford to upgrade and he had read once that every writer needed a good room.

As he approached the second floor, he noticed the corners of newspapers taped to the light blue wall. The ripped articles lay on the floor and he counted at least five different dusty footprints. He knocked on Teresa's door and waited. There was no answer and he knew she'd never see the rose if he left it. Continuing slowly up the stairs, he arrived at his flat and entered to the smell of freshly grilled meat and vegetables. He went to the kitchen and found Germano standing over the stove and stirring a sizzling pan. "Hey, dude," he said.

"Happy *Sant Jordi*." Johnny handed him the rose. "What you cooking?"

He took the flower and set it on the counter. "Some meat, potatoes and spinach."

"It smells good."

"I'm using some spices my mom sent from Africa. I'll leave you a little."

"Great. I'll do the dishes."

Germano turned off the stove and looked at Johnny. "You're less grumpy this afternoon."

"I just got offered my dream job of few hours and great pay."

"Doing what?"

"Teaching."

"I thought you were over it."

"I am. But it pays the bills, and now I'll have more time to write."

"Any ideas?"

"No, I'm going to my room to smoke a joint, listen to some music, and see what creative juices it stirs up."

Germano laughed. "I might join you."

"No problem."

His flat mate took a plate from the cupboard and piled on the food. "By the way, you know Jared Stewart?"

"The big guy who always goes to the Shamrock?"

"Yeah. That's him. He was killed the other week."

"No shit. Wow." Johnny had recently hooked up with his ex-girlfriend.

"Yep, by Port Olimpic."

"You know, it really doesn't surprise me with the life he lived." Johnny took a fork from the drawer and tried the food. The hot spices cleared his nose as an idea for a story formed in his mind. He would write about the seedy world of illegal tele-sales in Barcelona and introduce the world to the people behind it, also known as spankers.

CSI Barcelona

A mass of a man, his face twisted and twitching, stormed into the packed club at Port Olimpic. Towering over the party-goers grooving to the flashing lights and pulsating music, he wiped the sweat running into his eyes, squinted, and scanned the dance-floor. His sights fixed on a blond girl who stood at the bar. Steam rose off his head and he scowled. "Get outta my way," he growled shoving a kid with baggy jeans and braids to the side.

"¡Joder! ¿Qué te pasa, tio?" The boy shot back with a nod of the head. "¿Tienes algún problema?"

The kid stepped up with his chest out looking for a fight.

"Speak English." The brute smashed his forehead into the bridge of the boy's nose sending him screaming to the ground. Lifting his blood splattered head, the English man sneered, "Anyone else got a problem?"

The group picked up their friend and parted with a series of mumbled Spanish insults. Looking around the club, the bull of a man refocused on the girl at the bar, saw red at her talking to an American he knew, and charged. People bounced off him like dull spears against a thick hide as he raged towards his target. Two bouncers with bulging veins and inflated arms rushed in and tackled him, wrestling him to the ground. He was strong; they were stronger.

"Get the fuck off me," he shouted as they dragged him kicking and screaming across the dance-floor and threw him out into the pouring rain.

Dusting himself off, he stood and steamed. As he readied for a second charge, a shout from above got his attention. He looked up seeing only a black speck in the night sky. In less than a second the speck became a large brick and - before he had a chance to run - it was a piece of a concrete smashing into his head.

***

The flashing blue lights a top the navy and white hatch-back police cars mixed with the orange light from the yellow ambulances to bathe the crime scene in a gas-light green. Outside the closed clubs of the port, party-goers with smudged makeup and soaked shirts stood around and spoke to uniformed police-officers   Pulling down the brim of his cap and lifting up the hood of his black parka, Dr. Josep Caldet, Head Detective for the Department of Forensic Investigation for the Catalan police, marched through the driving rain to a taped off area where a representative from each of the three police forces stood.

"Grissom!" belted a young male officer in the fluorescent-yellow and dark-blue uniform of the *Guardia Urbana,* charged with protecting the city. "Glad you finally made it!"

The doctor winced and ignored the man, turning instead to a woman in the navy and crimson colors of the *Mossos d'Esquadra* who, like him, was in charge of the Catalan region. "So, what do we have here?"

"Looks like a piece of concrete fell from the boardwalk above," she told him.

He turned his attention away from the female officer and looked through his black designer glasses at the large man on the ground, the blood still flowing from his crushed skull.

"Do we know who he is?"

"No. But the bouncers think he's English. He picked a fight with some South Americans."

"Where's the coroner?"

"He's having a cup of coffee," answered a man in a dark military-looking uniform with a machine gun. He represented *la Policia Nacional* and the national police.

"I see." Looking up to the tall rectangular silhouette of the MAPFRE Insurance building, the falling rain pelted the lenses of his glasses and the doctor said, "In England, they say on a day like to today, 'It's raining cats and dogs' because in the past pets slept on the roofs and when it rained, they fell off."

"That's interesting, Doctor Caldet," replied the female officer.

"Yes, I thought so too." He took off his glasses, dried them with his sleeve and looked at the blurry young woman through his smudged lenses. "Although, tonight we must amend the phrase to 'It's raining concrete slabs'. And please, call me Josep or 'Pep' or 'Pepito,' anything but Grissom."

***

Under the bright lights of the stone and steel autopsy room located in the basement of the Bellvitge morgue, Dr. Josep "Pep" Caldet stood with his trusted leather folder under his arm. He looked at the corner, Francisco Lopez, in his blue smock and said, "Tell me, Paco."

"Well, the police report was right. Time of death was 2:30 in the morning. Also, it appears he was looking up at impact." The coroner pointed to the shattered nose, eye sockets and forehead of victim, now cleaned up and lying naked on a metal gurney between the two men.

"That's curious." Pep opened his folder and flipped through the sketches on the right side. He settled on one with the victim standing and the falling slab of concrete. Taking out a mechanical pencil, he clicked some lead and quickly adjusted the human figure's oval shaped face to look up. "Perhaps someone said something to get his attention?"

"Do we know who he is? He's obviously not Spanish. I would say English or German."

"English, and not yet."

"Figures. All the English like to do is come to Spain, get drunk and fight."

"I wouldn't say *all*. Have you ever been to England?"

"No. Who would want to? Terrible food and weather. Plus, the people are strange; they lack life. Spain is much better."

"That's a bit of a generalization, isn't it? It's like saying all Spanish take siestas."

"That's true of the people from the south. In *Catalunya*, we work too hard to sleep siestas."

"Except for the weekends, right?"

The coroner's brow lifted in confusion at the question. "Anyway, his blood alcohol level was three times the limit and he had enough cocaine in his system to have killed most men."

"Had he not been killed, would he have od'ed?"

"Doubt it. When I worked in the ER of the Hospital del Mar, I treated English men with twice these levels. Drinking and drugging seem to be part of their genetic make-up."

Pep said, "On that point, Paco, I would have to agree with you," closed his folder and left. He hated spending time in that cold place of death and talking to the coroner who was the two things he detested – opinionated and ignorant.

***

Back at his cozy and carpeted office more befitting a professor than a detective, Pep Caldet sat at his cluttered, wooden desk and reviewed the autopsy report. He still had no idea of who and why. A knock sounded on the door and he stopped reading. "Come in," he said as he stood to welcome the visitor.

It was the young female *Mosso* from earlier. "Hello doctor. I am Sergeant Montserrat Cubert."

"It's nice to see you again, Sergeant Cubert. Please sit. How I can help you?"

"Thank you and call me: 'Montse'." She sat down and looked at the framed pictures of the doctor, his wife and twin daughters. "You have a beautiful family."

"Thank you. I am very lucky, although right now my girls just finished university so now they are at the stage where all they do is ask for money. One is in Australia for a year and the other in London. I spoil them, but that's what happens when you grow up just after the civil war." He stopped and offered an apologetic grin. "I digress. What can you tell me about the victim?"

"His name is Jared Stewart. A drunken American girl id'ed him at the scene. Apparently she was the victim's ex-girlfriend and he was at the club looking for her."

"I see. Is she a suspect?"

"Everyone's a suspect right now, doctor."

"Please call me 'Pep'. I think we can rule her out."

"Why do you say that?"

"The piece of concrete was too big for one person to lift. Besides, the nearest construction debris was by the beach." He opened his leather folder and flipped to a sketch of how he imagined the crime taking place and continued, "Based on the time-line, Jared was killed shortly after being kicked out, which means the killers were waiting for him here." Using his mechanical pencil as a pointer, he showed Montse a group of tiny black figures standing in the shadow of the MAPFRE building.

"You're positive the brick was thrown and didn't simply fall?"

"Yes. Look..." He pointed the pencil at the other side of the folder and the meticulously drawn to scale scene with a curve tracing the trajectory of the falling slab from the promenade to Jared's head. "You see it fell too far from the edge to be an accident. Someone had to have helped it over."

"You're quite the artist."

"Thank you. It's my passion. Oh, I've also analyzed the slab and found some skin samples. It's the only physical evidence I could gather, I'm afraid." He closed the folder. "The rain corrupted most of the cigarette butts and the rough concrete makes getting a fingerprint impossible."

"Could it have been just a random attack?"

"Could be, but such incidences are rare here in Barcelona. As I'm sure you know, most violence is domestic in nature. Machismo is still, unfortunately, strong. Things are changing of course." He stopped and smiled. "But anyway, I'm digressing again. What do we know about Jared?"

"The British consulate was quick to call back. I guess he is the son of a well-to-do family."

"Perhaps Scotland Yard will get involved?"

"I doubt it. The victim isn't a cute, blond, blue-eyed toddler. Also, his ex-girlfriend said he was bad news and had a long list of enemies. He was what they call 'a spanker.'"

"A what?"

"*A spanker.*" Montse explained that the American girl wasn't forthcoming about exactly what Jared did, but she did provide the names of three English pubs the victim frequented. Her captain, however, said the main suspects were the group of South Americans and to follow that lead.

He could tell she wasn't convinced. "You don't agree?"

"No. My hunch tells me to follow up on Jared Stewart."

"Why don't you do that?"

"The captain doesn't like to be disobeyed."

"Well, at least check out the bars. We'll tell him it was my idea. I have an international forensics conference in Edinburgh next week and would like to practice my English anyway." It was a lie but there was something about this female officer Pep liked. Her desire to actually find the real culprits was refreshing when so many other officers he knew looked at policing as a civil service job and just punched the clock.

***

Pep always loved Barcelona the day after a rain. The stones of the buildings along the avenues sparkled and the sky above the green mountains was a clear blue, allowing for the bright yellow sun to shine. Today, however, he was too scared to notice. Gripping the door handle and with his head pinned back, he sat in a panic as Sergeant Montserrat Cubert's navy and white hatchback Seat weaved through the racing cars, scooters and buses on

Gran Via with its sirens blaring and lights flashing. "There hasn't been a kidnapping," he said through clenched teeth.

"Sorry."

"You know, there's no rush. This isn't a Hollywood movie."

"Yes, you're right. Sorry." Montse switched off the sirens and lights and pulled behind a black and yellow taxi. "I'm just anxious to solve this case."

"Patience my dear," he replied as they parked in front of a sand colored box-shaped church with a golden dome. Teenagers with dread-locks sitting in the dirt plaça quickly picked up their backpacks and disappeared to a cloud of hashish smoke at the sight of the white and blue police car.

Montse paid little attention to the spliff smoking kids as she got out of the car and slammed the door in frustration. "This is the third place on the list."

"Third time's a charm," said Pep.

***

Across from the church was bar with a green wooden doorway and a chalkboard of upcoming football matches posted on the outer wall. The inside was a dark and narrow before opening up onto large area at the back with small tables, stools and a large projector screen. By the front entrance was the open door to the kitchen where Pep and Montse took a seat and waved at a pale bearded kid with a pony-tail who worked behind the bar. "Whatkin I gitcha?" he said in mumbled English.

Mustering up some courage and remembering what his teacher had taught him, Pep answered, "One pint of Guinness please, mate."

"Doctor, we're on duty," Montse reprimanded him in Catalan.

He continued speaking English, "A Guinness clears the head. You should try one."

"Anything for me," Montse said incorrectly. "You espeak espanish?"

"No." The boy topped off the pint and handed it to the doctor.

Montse sighed in annoyance at having to speak a language that wasn't her own. "You know Jared Stewart?"

"Yeah, I know 'im. What's he done?"

The boy's words were a garbled series of noises that sounded as if he had a mouth full of marbles. She looked to the doctor and spoke to him in Catalan, "Have you understood him?"

"Yes, more or less." He sipped the rich stout and continued in English, "I love Guinness. This reminds me of when me and my family, we went to Ireland."

"Pep!" she snapped.

"Sorry." The doctor looked at the pony-tailed boy. "Can you tell me how long Jared be coming here?"

"He's *been* coming since before I started and that was a year ago."

He only caught some words. "I'm sorry. Could you repeat, please. And speak a little more slowly."

"One second. The owner's Spanish. Lemme go get him."

Montse watched the bartender disappear into the kitchen and then turned to Pep. "I don't understand. How can you come to this country, live and work and not learn the language? I can appreciate not learning Catalan if you are only here a short while, but at least *Castellano*."

"I imagine when you come to a foreign country, you tend to stick together."

"That's no excuse! If I lived in London, I would have to learn English."

"Yes, of course you're right, they should. I was just explaining why they don't." He sipped his beer. "Are you sure you don't want to try some?"

"Positive. Look, here comes the owner."

A barrel of a man with salt and pepper hair, the owner appeared more a retired boxer than the proprietor of a bar. "Hello, how can I help you?" he said.

Pep picked up on the Spanish accent that dropped the 'S' at the end of words. "From Andalucia?"

"I was born in Jaen, but grew up in Madrid. You're here about Jared Stewart?"

Montse seized control of the conversation. "Yes. What can you tell us about him?"

"He started coming almost two years ago. I think he's from London. A real hard case, but he's always well-behaved when he comes here. I make sure of it."

"What's a spanker?"

"You don't know?"

"No."

The bar owner snickered. "I'm surprised. It seems if an English person living here isn't a teacher or working on the boats, they're a spanker."

"Great," Montse said. "Mind telling us exactly what they are and what they do?"

Looking around the empty bar, he replied, "Okay, but please try to keep my name out of it."

"I can't promise. But if you don't tell me, I do guarantee an inspection to see if all your workers have the correct employment papers."

"Alright, alright. I'll tell you what I know," he sighed. His voice dropped to a whisper as he detailed the shady world of fraudulent tele-sales, otherwise known as *spanking*, which had taken root in Barcelona. Run mostly by men from the U.K., with a sprinkling of Irish,

65

Americans and Australians thrown in, they came to the city and opened offices of nothing but desks and telephones. From these locations, they called their home countries and peddled fake stocks and shares to mostly the old, lonely and naive.

The bosses, like Jared, were long time veterans who had fled the U.K. after authorities cracked down on their illicit activities at the beginning of the nineties. They then bounced around to different European cities, setting up spank shops until the local police caught wind, making it time to leave. Barcelona was the perfect location. The general lack of English meant they could conduct their business with little fear of the Spanish authorities understanding their conversations. The great quality of life made it a good recruiting tool while working in sterling made rents cheap with the Euro getting seventy cents to the pound. Amazed at what she had heard, Montse said, "Isn't that illegal?"

"Of course it is," replied the owner.

"Then how can it be happening here?"

"You're the police. You tell me. I suppose because they don't target Spanish people and pay cash for everything. Like the mafias of *El Raval*."

His interest peaked by this unknown seedy side of Barcelona, Pep asked, "And why do they call them spankers?"

"Because of their ability on the phones. A regular of mine said, they literally, verbally beat the person on the other end down until they agree to buy. First time investors always get a great return and soon they put their whole savings in and by the end they have nothing."

"I can't believe anyone would fall for them," Montse said shaking her head in disbelief.

"All of these guys have the gift of gab and zero conscience."

"Tragic," replied the doctor as he finished his beer. "How do they get the numbers?"

"Just like any other tele-sales business - they buy them from the multinational banks like Citibank and Barclays."

"Why haven't you called and told us about them?" Montse asked.

"Because they're also good and loyal customers. Each one spends two hundred a night and with an Irish bar opening on every corner, competition is steep."

"Did he have friends?"

"Look behind you. Do you see that picture?" Stuck on the wall were photos of customers in different states of inebriation depending on the number of empty pint glasses on the table. A sun-burned Jared Stewart surrounded by a group of equally red friends was in the middle of the collage. "That's his crew from last year. Some are still here, but most have gone. He seems to have new people every month."

Montse turned from the pictures on the wall and faced the owner. "Do they come in often?"

"They'll probably be in for the Champions League match tonight. They're all Chelsea fans."

"Great. Can we take this picture?"

"Sure. By the way, is Jared in some kind of trouble?"

"Jared Stewart was killed last night."

The owner's face sank at the unexpected news. "You think his friends did it?"

"We don't know, but if they come in tonight, act normal, okay?"

Watching Montse stand to leave, Pep was impressed by her strength and character. Police work was obviously her life and he envied that. He had never wanted to go into medicine. He hated death but his father had wanted him to be a doctor saying there was no life for an artist. Pep never had the courage to stand up to him, fearing disappointing the man who had lost so much in the Civil War, a man who worked two jobs so his son could get the best education. If he couldn't be the next great Spanish painter, then he would settle for being a detective like *Hercule Poirot* from the Agatha Christie books he enjoyed reading as a child. And, while his job made him proud, he felt no passion for it like the young female detective he followed out the door.

***

Back at the crime scene in the shadow of the charcoal MAPFRE building, Pep looked across the sailboats of the populated marina to the turquoise Mediterranean Sea. He thought how none of this district had existed before the Olympic Games in 1992. For so long this area had been a derelict industrial zone left for the gypsies. Now it had a sparkling statue of a bronze fish designed by Gehry, beaches for people to bake on in the summer and the building at whose base he stood. With his folder open, he sketched sergeant Montserrat Cubert as she talked to the club staff by the construction debris near a pier where the sea met the beach. Pointing up at Pep, she paused, waved and smiled. He slipped his pencil in the breast pocket of his shirt and waved back before closing the folder, tucking it under his arm and walking down the steps.

"Any luck?" he asked meeting her near the club where Jared was killed.

The beaming expression on her face revealed the answer. "Yes! Three people remember hearing a group of English people shouting by the beach and then later after the brick fell," she explained excitedly before her small mouth pursed in annoyance. "I told the captain to canvass the boardwalk to see if there were any witnesses, but he said it was an accident and went to have a coffee."

"That's the easy way to do it."

"It seems all the idiots become bosses."

"Until they fail. The only problem is how long it takes and how much damage is done in the interim."

Montse groaned.

"I know, but it is what it is," Pep replied. "Most people call me Grissom and think I can solve any crime and, that like him, I study bugs. Before I got irritated and told them, 'I kill cockroaches and I'm terrified of spiders'." He looked out to the white yachts of the marina and gestured angrily at the calm sea. "Still, they call me fucking Grissom and yell when I don't solve every case. 'This isn't America,' I tell them. We don't have fancy computers. This is Spain. I have a five-year-old piece of shit that freezes if I open more than two programs and have to fill out three forms for every request."

The rising tone of his voice and the rapid beating of his heart gave him pause and he took a deep breath. Turning to Montse and offering a weak smile of a man who had reluctantly come to a decision, he said, "Now I stay calm because it does me no use getting angry and it's bad for my heart."

The puzzled Sergeant replied, "I see...I think. The good news is we have enough to bring in Jared's friends tonight."

"Yes, that is good news. When you bring them in, call me and I will get a DNA sample to match."

"Would you like to come along? It's your investigation after all."

"Well, there hasn't been another murder and I can't write a report until this is solved. So, yes, thank you."

"Don't mention it. Oh, by the way - did you read about that guy who attacked the civil servant with a ticket dispenser?"

"Yes, I don't know what's happening to Barcelona. No one seems to have any patience anymore and everyone is fighting with each other." Looking out to the yachts in the marina, he wondered what it would be like to escape this crazy city and spend his life at sea like his fisherman grandfather who had taught him how to draw. Every day it seemed like a better idea if only he didn't have two daughters to support.

***

Back at the police station, officers in pale-blue, short-sleeved shirts stood around wooden desks, drinking coffee and chatting about that night's Champions League football match between *Barça* and Chelsea. Their conversation loud and animated, Pep said, "It all depends if Messi is healthy or not."

"Grissom, you like football?" shouted one of the officers, a fresh faced recruit looking to impress the others.

"Yes, I enjoy a good match or when *Espanyol* play."

"You're a *perico*, Grissom? But they're fascists."

"Are they?"

"Yes. *Barça* is the true team of *Catalunya*. *¡Es mas que un club!*"

"I cannot disagree with the beauty of their football. But tell me, why do *Barça* supporters only shout and applaud when they win, but whine and criticize when they lose? Do you support the team or the winning?" Pep looked into the smooth face of a young officer who seemed less full of himself and added, "They say the quietest place in Spain is Camp Nou with *Barça* trailing nil-one, which I believe was the result last year when we played and beat you."

The recruit cursed and stormed out the door.

"You put him in his place, *Grissom*," whispered Montse as they opened the door and walked into captain's office.

Taller than the average Spaniard with massive hands, broad shoulders and a bushy black mustache, Captain Xavier Fernandez cut an imposing figure as he stood up from behind his desk and stared at the female police officer. "How can I help you, Cubert?"

"I've been following up on some leads regarding the Jared Stewart case."

"Have you been in *Poble Sec* with the other officers looking for the *sudacas*?"

"No, sir. I think he was killed by a group of English men."

"I know the English are hooligans, but what makes you think that?"

"The evidence, sir." She filled him in about finding out the location where the suspects were likely to be later that night, the witness confirmation of a group of English at the beach, and the DNA sample Pep found on the brick.

Her captain's dark brown eyes narrowed and his busy eyebrows become one as he scowled. "I thought I said the *sudacas* were our primary suspects."

Pep stepped in. "I believe the correct term is South Americans and they still are. We just need to rule out the English angle."

The captain's eyes remained fixed on Montse. "You can use two officers off the clock."

Doing her best not to smile, she replied, "Thank you, sir."

He continued to glare at her in a uni-brow rage as if he was thinking of ways to make her pay. "But, Sergeant, if I catch you going behind my back and disobeying orders again, I will have your ass. Do we understand each other?"

"Yes, sir."

His angry gaze set on Pep. "As for you, doctor, aren't you a little old to be playing detective?"

"One is never too old to solve a murder." Pep grinned smugly as he watched the captain shake with a fury he knew could never be released on him, not even verbally because according to Spanish law, Head Detective outranked Captain making Pep his boss.

***

The owner of the bar's face went from smiley and jovial to blank and terrified at the sight of Sergeant Montserrat Cubert dressed in jeans and a t-shirt, Pep Caldet in slacks and a cardigan and two more male officers in their civilians entering. "You're back?" he asked.

"Yes, but stay calm," replied Montse as they sat at the top of the bar by the front door and kitchen entrance. An hour before kickoff saw only a few couples sitting at the small tables in the main area.

"Are you here to arrest those English boys?"

"We want to talk to them at the station. What's the matter?"

"It's just – I don't want any trouble, you know?"

"Don't worry, that's why we're here early; we'll grab them and leave. What I need for you to do is nod when they come in and stay calm. Can you do that?"

"Yes."

"Good. Now go act normal. And remember, take it easy." Turning to her left, she spoke to an officer who was short and stocky with cropped black hair, "Thanks for coming, Pau. I owe you one."

His tough guy expression softened. "How about that dinner I've been after?"

"How about a coffee to start?" She patted his bicep bulging underneath a tight polo-shirt. "Been working out I see."

He blushed.

"We should order something while we wait," suggested the other male office, Alfonso, a wiry man in an Adidas tracksuit, his spiked hair glistening from too much gel.

"Yes, a good idea," replied Pep. "I think I'll have a Guinness."

Montse looked at him disapprovingly.

"What? You're worse than my daughters. Fifteen years ago, we would have been drinking a bottle of wine while we waited. Besides, these men aren't armed."

"I think *we* would've been you three, with me at home cooking and cleaning," Montse corrected him. "But I suppose one won't hurt. We are undercover after all." Calling over the owner, she ordered a round of Guinness.

Observing a rail thin man with a square head at the other side of the bar, Alfonso said, "Man, the English can drink. That guy's on his third bottle in ten minutes."

"You're right," replied Pau. "I did a cross-training for a month with the Manchester police department and the weekends there are crazy. It's cold and raining and people are stumbling drunk in the streets, girls with nothing but miniskirts and halter-tops and boys wearing nothing but blazers. Everyone is fighting."

Montse shuddered at the image. "It sounds horrible."

"I suppose it does, but when you stay and live there, you see another part of their life and you understand a little why."

"I guess so. But it seems really sad."

The front door creaked open and the chatter of English stopped their conversation. Looking out the corner of her eye, Montse saw that it was a mixed-group of boys and girls with *Barça* football scarves.

"Here you go," said the owner handing them their four pints. "They're on the house."

Montse took a sip. Her mouth curled and her face contorted in disgust. "This is horrible! It's so bitter."

"It's an acquired taste," said Pep as the trickle of people entering the bar through the creaky door became a steady stream.

The place filled to the talking-heads of Sky Sports football hyping the match as the crowd of mainly *Barça* supporters, wearing the team's navy blue and burgundy colors, made their way through the bar in search for an increasingly hard to find free seat. None of the people matched the suspects from the picture on the wall.

After a few minutes, the door flung open again. "Blue is the color, football is the game," rang through the bar in a booming, out of tune chorus. The owner's face went white telling them all they needed to know.

As the three *Mossos* unlocked their holsters, Pep turned to look to see what confronted them. One of the men was big – in a fat, non-muscular way – and wore a blue Chelsea football jersey; the other had ginger hair and looked like he was fresh out of high-school. Putting years of training into practice, the three officers pushed away from the bar and closed in on the two young men while Pep sat and watched.

The muscular Sergeant Pau Llobert put his hand on the big one's shoulder. "Excuse me."

"What you want?"

"We are the *Mossos d'Esquadra* and would like that you come with us."

"Fuck off. I'm here to watch..."

Before he finished his sentence, Pau grabbed his wrist, spun him around, and twisted his arm up with one hand, slamming the boy's head on the bar counter with the other. The move was done with such speed and power that it dazed the younger boy, who turned to Montse and extended his hands to be cuffed, rather than suffer the same fate. With their suspects apprehended, the officers led them to their cars parked in front of the domed church where the sweet smell of hashish still lingered in the air.

***

They had been at the police station nearly an hour when an exasperated Montse approached Pep who sat doodling at her desk. "Doctor, Pau is in with the fat one. Do you mind talking to the young one? He doesn't speak Spanish, Alfonso and I don't understand him."

"Sure," he replied, standing and walking into the green brick interrogation room where the young boy waited under a light so bright it made his head start to hurt. He pulled out a plastic chair and sat across from the boy. "Hello, I am Doctor Josep Caldet. You are Andy Johnson, correct?"

"Yes."

"You know why you are here?"

"No."

"Because we know you killed Jared Stewart."

"No, we didn't."

"We found some of skin on the cement. Please show me your hands."

"Don't I get a lawyer?"

"No." The doctor snatched the boy's handcuffed wrists and looked at his scraped palms. He let go and shook his head. "Why did you do it, Andy? Tell me and it will mean that you spend less time in prison."

"We didn't do nuffin."

Pep sat back and studied the freckled baby face of the suspect. He decided on a new approach. "Tell me, Andy, how much time you work for Jared?"

"I was one of the first people he brought over last year, why?"

"You were close, no?"

"I guess. He always let you know who was the boss, though."

"And who's the boss now?"

"Dunno. I imagine the top-earner will take over."

"Is that you?"

The boy laughed. "No."

"What happens to the ones who don't earn enough?"

"They look for new work."

"Is that why you killed him, Andy?"

The boy's tiny green eyes widened in surprise at the line of questioning. "Wha'?"

"I understand that there is always new people coming, no? That must create much pressure to sell."

"Yeah, so?"

Pep thought about his next question and decided it was time for a little deceit. "Your friend says it was your idea to kill Jared to avoid getting sacked."

"No, he didn't. Besides, it was 'im that was about to lose 'is desk. I 'ad another month to prove myself."

"I don't understand."

"You wanna fucking know what working with Jared was like, mate?" Andy explained how, when they first arrived, Jared gave them the best leads of pensioners that hadn't been picked over and called thousands of times. The problem was a person had to stay in the top five on the sales board to keep receiving these golden phone numbers, which was almost impossible given many in the office could convince a dread-locked Jamaican to join the right wing British National Party. Andy and his friends weren't that adept on the phone so they ended up getting pages of paper so marked up it was difficult to make out the telephone numbers. "But that's fucking with a geezer's livelihood, innit?"

Pep didn't understand many of these strange words or exactly what the suspect described. It was unlike any English he had ever heard. "More or less," he replied. "What I don't understand is, why not go to another company?"

"'Cos Jared wudda made sure no other place hired us. He was a cunt like that." The boy paused and his baby face hardened into the criminal he was. "But more than that, he was kicking us out of the flat the company rented and we wudda 'ad to go back to fucking England."

"Why not look for another flat and a new type of job so you can stay?"

"'Cos I don't speak fucking Spanish, mate."

"You killed him to stay in Barcelona?"

"I wanna lawyer."

*****

Walking out the interrogation room, a weary Pep found Sergeant Montserrat Cubert leaning against the automatic coffee machine with a plastic cup in hand. "It was definitely them," he said.

"Did he confess?"

"No, but I know the motive."

"That's great. Why so down?"

"Because I'm afraid for my city."

"What do you mean?"

"Fifteen years ago gypsies were our biggest problem and we understood them. Now we have foreigners doing things we don't understand, men attacking state employees. It is what it is, I suppose, but Barcelona is changing and I don't think it's for the better." He stopped and half smiled. "But don't listen to me, I'm just a tired old-man who must go home."

"Come on, Pep. It's not that bad. At least we're not in Las Vegas or New York or Miami with serial killers and gangsters and nuclear terrorists where everyone has machine guns."

"I suppose you're right."

"So, can I call you the next time I need an extra pair of eyes or someone who speaks English?"

"Yes, I would like that very much." He rethought the offer. "But hopefully not too soon, because that would mean another crime has occurred in Barcelona and I'd rather it stay calm and quiet."

El Funcionario

On the top floor of one of the majestic buildings along Passeig de Gracia, a man enters a lawyer's office. He finds his prospective legal representative, not eagerly awaiting a potential client, but instead sitting at a large oak desk reading a paper. He coughs to get his attention. The lawyer licks his finger and flips the page.

"Excuse me," says the man staring at a person not much older than he, but with a full head of black hair and a round face of someone who eats well.

Slowly folding the paper along its creases before carefully setting it down, the lawyer stands and comes around his desk. "Yes? How can I help you?" he replies with the intonation and pronunciation of an educated man as he extends his hand to welcome the man.

The lawyer's grip is like a military officer's and the man flinches in pain. "I have a five o'clock appointment. I'm the one who attacked the state employee."

"Yes, I know who you are. I saw you on the news." The lawyer lets go of a limp wrist and motions to a small wooden chair on the other side of the large oak desk. "Please take a seat."

"Thanks." The man carefully removes his faded blazer, hangs it on the back of the chair, making sure it's perfectly straight and even before he sits down. The wall to his right is papered with prestigious diplomas. "You have to study a lot to be a lawyer, don't you?"

"Yes, and take many, many exams." The lawyer sits down in a leather wingback chair and opens a drawer. "So, tell me. What on earth possessed you to attack someone? You don't look the type."

"It's a long story."

The lawyer takes out a leather folder and a silver pen. "Well, if you want me to represent you, you'll have to tell me, because right now you're facing ten years in prison for attacking a state employee."

"Ten years! But the maximum sentence possible is twenty!" The man pictures his wife's volcanic temper erupting at the news.

"Actually, thirty, if you're a terrorist," explains the lawyer. "But the fact is according law X.564.P.907/N, a government employee is in essence an extension of the state. And as such, any attack on them is punishable by a minimum sentence of ten years in prison." He reminds the man that – as people, who must not only pass a series of complicated worded exams for their chosen government position, but also place in the top five percentile – *funcionarios* are afforded the full legal protections of Spanish law, the same ones given to another state employee – the president. "Perhaps, even more so because he can lose an election, while not going to work for months won't get a *funcionario* fired."

"I know, I know." The man doesn't need to be reminded about the perks of state employment. Like most of his friends, he's wanted to be a *funcionario* since childhood. But, like most adults, despite studying the thousands of arcane rules and regulations written in Spanish legalese all day, every day, for years, he still hasn't passed the series of exams known as *las oposiciones* to reach his dream.

"Okay, so I hit a state employee. But don't you think ten years is a little much? For fuck's sake, the pedophile in L'Eixample got out in six. And that was after his fourth conviction!"

"That was due to good behavior. We're not America. We don't send people away for life or execute them."

"But six years for raping a kid?"

The lawyer picks up the pen and opens the folder. "We might be able to reduce your sentence. But first you must tell me what happened."

"Where should I start?" says the man.

"The beginning is always good," replies the lawyer.

The man coughs to clear his throat. "You know that new law that went into effect last January?"

"Which one?"

"The one that requires residents of Barcelona to get a special identification card for certain city services?"

The lawyer nods and writes. "Law 20.210-19X."

"Yes, I believe that's the number. How did you know it so quickly?"

"I'm a lawyer. I must know the law."

"Yes, of course. But it's truly remarkable." The man shakes his head in admiration. "You must be very intelligent."

"It takes a lot of studying."

"I imagine so. I wanted to be a lawyer, but my test scores in high school placed me at a science and math university." The man looks around the office which is twenty times the size of his cubicle. "So I got a degree in economics and now I work as an accountant."

"A respectable job."

"Yes, I suppose. But the salaries aren't much."

"Enough to live on, isn't it?"

"Barely." The man looks at the well-fed face of the lawyer and says, "But nothing like yours."

The lawyer grins. "I think we're getting off track. We were discussing the new law and why you attacked somebody."

"Yes, of course." The man moves his numb ass on the hard chair to get some feeling back before continuing his story, "So, I got a letter from city hall at the end of November reminding me that I hadn't filed the paperwork for my new number yet."

"Why did you wait so long to do it?"

"Because I don't have time for anything anymore," says the man, flailing his arms as he details hectic days that start at seven and finish at midnight with the only time to relax being when he sleeps.

The lawyer's expression turns serious and he sets down the pen. "This law applies to *all* residents of Barcelona – even to me – so we all must find the time to fulfill it."

"I suppose so." The man stands to stretch, goes to a window and opens the green curtain. Across the street is la Casa Milà shimmering in the late afternoon sun. "Although, I still don't understand why I need yet another number and another card."

"Aside from the €5,000 fine?"

"Yes."

"As an official Barcelona resident, you get a discounted rate on transportation passes and for most sights, like the Sagrada Familia and Parc Güell."

Turning away from the window, the man stares down the lawyer. "I was raised in this city and all my family lives here. We don't sightsee."

"What!" The lawyer slams his pen on the desk in amazement. "But Barcelona is the most beautiful city in the world!"

"Yes, it's the best, like its football club. But I've already told you, *I don't have time.*" The man returns to the hard wooden chair and huffs. Reaching in his pocket, he pulls out a pack of cigarettes. "May I?"

"Of course." The lawyer slides a blue crystal ashtray on the desk to him. "So, you received this letter?"

"Yes." The man lights a cigarette and explains the bureaucratic process in Barcelona.

***

The first stop was his local municipal office in the L'Eixample district where he was to present documentation proving he was a resident and get the form. After filling it out in blue - not black - ink, he was then to take it to the Catalan regional office in Drassanes to have it stamped and signed. Once finished there, he was supposed to return to L'Eixample and receive an additional signature verifying that it had been signed before registering his new number with the Spanish authorities near *Estació de França*. After doing all that, he was to return to L'Eixample and submit the form. He could expect a card with his new number in three to six months.

***

The lawyer finishes taking notes, shrugs his shoulders. "Okay. What's the big deal? One for the city, the autonomy and the country."

"Doesn't that seem like a bit much for a number that offers me nothing?" The man tosses the spent butt in the ashtray.

"As I keep telling you, the law is the law." The lawyer thinks and says, "What I don't understand is, why not just pay someone to do it? It's only seventy-five Euros. That's what I do."

"Money's tight."

The lawyer closes the folder. "If you don't mind me asking, how do you expect to pay for *my* services?"

"Don't worry. My family has offered me a loan."

"Continue then." The lawyer reopens the folder.

The man cannot get comfortable in the chair, so he stands again and heads to the back of the office where a Picasso print hangs above a plush couch. "Anyway, I took some time off work to get started and went to the L'Eixample office around ten," he says sitting down on the soft cushions, feeling comfortable for the first time that afternoon.

"They close at two. Why not go earlier?" The lawyer jots down a couple of words before shouting, "And, please, sit in the seat. I can barely hear you."

The man takes a couple of candies from a bowl on a stone coffee table before slowly standing and returning to the desk.

"Well, I wanted a lie-in." He bites on the hard caramel and chews. "I also found it doesn't matter how early you get there, either way you aren't leaving before noon with everyone and their mother wanting to be the first to arrive."

"Hmm… You know, thinking about it." The lawyer looks up, smiles in surprise and thrusts his arm at the man to congratulate him. "I believe you're right."

"I imagine you never have to do deal with the Spanish bureaucracy, do you?"

"Like I said, I pay people to do it."

The man looks into the small brown eyes almost hidden from view behind the fat cheeks of the lawyer and curses God for not being smart enough to pass the tests to work in the highly paid legal profession or as a state employee. He pops a second candy in his mouth and crunches. "I see."

The lawyer readies to write again. "Please, continue – You're at the L'Eixample office."

"Okay, so far so good. I'm in and out in just forty-five minutes, so I take advantage to fill the form out and head to the Drassanes office."

"Did you drive?"

"No, I left my car at the office parking lot. It's too expensive to park in the city-center anymore."

The shocked lawyer stops writing and looks at the man as if he has just said he drove a Seat when it was the crown jewel of the Spanish automobile industry, and not a subsidiary of Audi. "You took the metro? I haven't ridden it since my university days."

The man lights a second cigarette. "Well, until Plaça Catalunya. I walked down Las Ramblas."

"Why didn't you just change lines?"

"You really don't ride it much, do you? It's like being one rat among hundreds in an underground maze of tunnels and steps."

The lawyer roars with laughter and leans back in his chair. "That's a bit of a poetic exaggeration, don't you think? You almost sound *Andaluz*. After all, thousands of people ride the metro every day and no one goes crazy and attacks people."

The man's teeth grit and his nostrils flare like an angry donkey. The label *Andaluz* stings for he is a proud, hardworking Catalan from the north and not some lazy southern Spaniard from Andalucia who only sings, dances and kills bulls. He takes a deep drag of nicotine to calm down.

"I suppose so. But it does add to the general level of stress. Don't you think?"

The lawyer's tiny brown eyes squint and his round face reddens in anger. "We all live with stress. Do you think I don't have stress in my life?"

"You're a lawyer. You're rich. You can buy anything."

"Not anything. I'm not Bill Gates."

"No. But I imagine you have a nice apartment in Barcelona and one in the mountains."

The lawyer blinks and says, "By the sea, actually. And let me tell you something - it's not easy paying for them, plus my children's private school and my new Mercedes."

Extinguishing the cigarette, the man looks at the sweating lawyer and replies, "You don't have to buy them."

The lawyer takes a deep breath and stands up from his comfy wingback chair. He goes to the window and opens it. The blasting horns and revving scooters seven stories below fill the room like it's on the ground floor. "We live in a democratic society now and I pay taxes, so I can spend my money as I like," he shouts to be heard over the noise of the street before returning to his seat for his closing argument, "If you don't like it, elect new politicians. Would you rather return to the time of Franco?"

The man is aghast at the accusation. "Of course not! No real Catalan would ever dare think such a thing."

"Good. Now hurry up. We've been talking for nearly an hour and I have a tennis match at seven." The lawyer's face remains stern as he picks up the pen to write again.

"Okay." The man doesn't know if he wants this lawyer to represent him, but so far, he's been the one with the most certificates and diplomas and the only non-*Castellano* or Argentinean. He lights another smoke and continues, "So, I get to the Drassanes office and take a ticket. The place is packed. Finally, two hours later, my number is called."

"So, what happened?

The man takes a long drag and exhales. "I walk up to the counter and the young guy working takes the form, the documents and my I.D. He says not a word for five minutes, just looks. Then he says: 'I need your income-tax statements too'. "He taps the cigarette hard over the ashtray. "'Where does it say that?' I say, and he recites some new law like it was a pledge."

Bellowing laughter comes from the lawyer. "You hit him for having an attitude? Have you ever met a pleasant *funcionario*?"

The man smokes and seethes as he starts to see red. "Are you laughing at me?"

"Of course not! But it's not easy dealing with the public every day."

"Nor is my job, where I actually have to work eight hours and can be fired for not producing."

"Don't you have a full-time work contract?"

"Of course, but I've only been there a year." The man explains, being eight months shy of his two year anniversary, when according to Spanish law, the cost of laying off contracted employees almost doubles from twenty-six to forty days paid for each year worked.

"Ah, I see." The lawyer's face conveys sympathy for the first time. "What happened after the boy rejected you?"

Mashing the smoldering butt in the ashtray as he relives the frustration, the man says, "I went to work, got yelled at by my boss and returned the next day to find the ticket machine broken and a long line."

"Did you wait?" The lawyer furiously scribbles notes.

"Hell no! Things are iffy at my company and I didn't want to arrive any later than I had to."

The lawyer stops and looks up from the folder. "What do you mean *iffy*?"

"Well, our head office in Madrid is looking to cut costs with the economic crisis and rumor has it Barcelona is first to go under the knife."

"It's always the same," shouts the lawyer, throwing the pen on the desk in disgust, watching it bounce off and hit the floor. "Madrid keeps everything and leaves us shit."

The man could not have said it better. "I know! To hell with the Socialists. They're no better than the PP. I'm voting for the Catalan Independence Party next election."

"You must be kidding. Their leader was born in Aragón. He's not even a true Catalan. Stick with who we have." The lawyer takes a pencil from a cup. " Just look at how much Barcelona has grown."

"Yeah, but for whom? My children won't be able to afford to live here. My wife and I can barely do it with two salaries."

Biting his lip, the lawyer ponders the question. He readies to resume note-taking, "So what happened next?"

The man lights yet another smoke. "I waited a week until my boss went on a business trip and tried again."

"And?"

"The same little shit from the last time said I had to pay a five Euro fee." The man snaps an almost full cigarette in half as he puts it out.

"That's not much."

"You're right but I only had a twenty. I asked him if he had change and he said 'No' and 'Next' without stamping the form."

"So you hit him?"

The man pauses and remembers the day. He calms down. "No. I would have, but a nice lady offered to lend me the money. I gave him a piece of my mind, though."

"Good for you. And?"

The man readies to light another smoke and stops. He crushes it in his hand and squeezes it like a stress ball as he speaks, "When I get to the L'Eixample office, the clerk tells me that the son of a bitch didn't initial the seal and to go back." He opens his palm and lets the loose tobacco and wrinkled paper fall in the quickly filling ashtray.

The lawyer laughs at his show of strength. "Easy there my friend. It wasn't their fault."

Dusting the tobacco off his hands, the man wonders who exactly this lawyer is supposed to represent. "Yeah, you're right. But, I was starting to get a bit paranoid that the guy had it in for me."

"I see." The lawyer writes a single word in his note book. "Continue, please."

In need of some air, the man stands and goes to the window where he watches the darkening sky of dusk and smells the exhaust fumes from rush hour traffic. "Anyway, what was supposed to originally be a four day process was turning into five days, if I was lucky."

"What's one more day?" The lawyer sets down his pen and closes the folder.

Anger runs up the man's legs, through his stomach and hits his heart. "I tell you why," he says, spinning away from the window and facing the lawyer, the red film of rage coming down over his eyes like dripping paint on a wall. "Because my asshole boss is on me about missing work and I'm not getting home until nine or ten trying to make up for it."

"That's only an hour later than me."

The man looks into the round face and tiny eyes of the lawyer and sees a brown pig. He wants to smack the son of a bitch and carve him up with the letter opener on the desk like a leg of *Jamon Iberico*. He knows his wife will explode into a foot stomping and plate throwing tantrum if she gets another call from the police.

"Do you have children?" asks the man.

"Yes, I already told you. Two," replies the lawyer.

"And, your wife doesn't mind you coming home late?"

"No, she doesn't work and we have a nanny."

The man's brown eyes turn emerald green with envy at the lawyer's success, the feelings of jealousy dulling and trumping his anger. God how he wished he were rich. "Well, we can't afford that luxury, so when I get home late, my children are asleep and my wife's in a mood that'd put the fear of God in a wild game hunter."

"Yes, my wife has a temper too. It's that Spanish blood." The lawyer stands up and puts his arm around the man as he leads him away from the open window. "I think you need a drink."

"I need a whiskey."

"Atta boy! A man after my own heart." The lawyer pats the man enthusiastically on the back before pushing him towards the hard wooden chair. "Now – Sit down."

"You have whiskey?"

"Do I have whiskey?" The lawyer struts to a standing wooden bar in the corner of the office. "I've got one of the finest single-malt Scotches sold."

"Really?"

"Yes. My family and I went to Edinburgh last year." The lawyer pours two tumblers from a crystal carafe.

The man sits down and says, "My wife and I went to England once before the kids. I hated it."

"It isn't Spain. That's for sure," seconds the lawyer as he hands the man a half full tumbler before returning to his wingback chair. "*Salut.*"

"*Salut.*" The man clinks glasses and takes sip.

The lawyer smacks his lips and lets out a satisfied 'ah.' "A fine whiskey, isn't it? It's the Highland water and malting process that makes it so special and expensive. The bottle cost me over a hundred Euros."

The man doesn't notice the difference between it and the one he usually buys at the store for a tenth of the price. "I normally like it with coke."

"Don't tell a Scot that." The lawyer's lips straighten into a mocking grin.

"Why, they don't drink whiskey and coke?"

"Never mind." The lawyer sips, smacks his lips and lets out another long 'ah' of contentment. Opening the folder, he reads his notes, "So, you were having a bad week at work and home and a frustrating time with some *funcionarios* over a law you didn't agree with." He pauses and smiles. "I think it's safe to say most people have probably suffered moments like this. This is Spain. It is what it is. What do you expect? The *funcionario's* job is to find problems where there are none."

"I know. I know. But even you will have to agree what I tell you next is shear provocation."

The lawyer perks up and takes the pencil. "I'm all ears."

The man gulps his whiskey like it's a shot and feels the burn as it travels down to his gut. He shivers, lights a smoke and continues with his story, "Since I needed the signature or I would have to start the whole process over, I went back to the Drassanes office and waited in line." He explains how he waits for over an hour until his number is finally called. He walks up to the counter with the form and a folder stuffed with a copy of every piece of documentation from his birth certificate to his most recent income-tax statement.

The person working is not the guy, but a girl, and she takes the piece of paper and slowly looks it over front to back three times, reading the fine print twice. Again, another long pause, before she informs him with the relish of a waiter telling an obnoxious customer that their credit card is declined, 'Sorry, sir, I obviously can't initial something I didn't stamp. You'll have to see my colleague who's working on the second floor'.

Grabbing the edge of the desk, the lawyer braces himself for the answer to the following question, "You didn't hit a woman, did you? It's not like it was even ten years ago, when there was no punishment. That's a real no-no now. And five years in jail."

"No. I waited another fucking forty minutes in a different line." The man grinds the burning cigarette against the bottom of the ashtray as if it were the boy's spotty face. "So, as you can imagine, I wasn't in the best of moods when I finally got to the little shit and asked him to please initial."

"What happened next?"

"Again, I get another long pause before he abruptly explains that, due to not working in that capacity today, he's not authorized to initial the stamp and to come back Monday. And that's when I lost it."

"What do you mean, *you lost it*?"

Taking a deep breath, the man pulls out another cigarette before deciding he has smoked enough and slipping it back. "To tell you the truth, I don't remember much," he says recalling the absurdity of the moment with the detachment of a spectator. "I shouted, '*I shit in the milk of your whore of a mother,*' and went for the ticket dispenser."

The man stops and tries to piece together exactly what happened that fateful day. "Everything went red after that and the next thing I know – I'm getting tackled to the ground by security and the *funcionario* is holding the top of his head and crying."

"And the ticket dispenser?"

"Ripped off its stand and by his station." The man taps his bony chest and it echoes. "Look, I'm not a hard guy. I really don't know how I did it."

The lawyer stops writing and chews on the end of a pencil as he thinks. "Well, I must say, it does seem like you had a bit of really bad luck. I could probably get you a five year sentence." He glances down at his notes and sees "crazy" written in large letters. "On account of acute mental distress. It's a bit of a reach and you'll have to see a psychiatrist."

"Five years!"

"With good behavior, you'll be out in a one."

"Can't you get me off completely? What would a normal assault charge get?"

"A first time offense? Maybe a month."

"You can't get me that?" says the man.

"The law is the law," replies the lawyer. "And it must be followed to the strictest letter, otherwise we have anarchy. And the fact is, you attacked a state employee."

"Haven't you been listening to a word I said? He provoked me!"

The lawyer smacks the table with the folder and says, "Look, even if you were innocent, which you aren't, it makes no difference. The law clearly says a state employee is always in the right." He offers an anecdote of a woman who is hit by a speeding police car while crossing a street. The light is green and there is no crime that necessitates such haste, nor are sirens used. However, as they are state employees and she is just a citizen, they are clear of all charges. She, meanwhile, has to pay for all for all damages to the squad car that knocks her over and breaks her hip on the way to crashing into a bus stop.

The man remembers hearing the story on the nightly news and stares at diplomas on the wall. The blood flows to his legs as he stands and slowly goes to the window one final time. *Casa Milà* is awash in the yellow spotlights of night. He thinks about how he has never visited it and about how pointless it has been to even believe he could take on a state employee. It doesn't matter that they are petty, incompetent and possibly mentally disturbed, given their glee in denying people and making everyone's lives miserable. The law is the law. The *funcionario* is right and the man wrong. I should have been more patient, he thinks before turning around and facing his future legal counsel who is busy packing a duffel bag with a change of clothes, but no racket. The man sighs in defeat, "What's the next step?"

The lawyer offers a sympathetic smile and zips the bag. "See my assistant this week, pay my retainer, and pick up a form. You'll then have to go to the judicial office near the Borne before taking it to your local municipal office in L'Eixample."

The man doesn't flinch at the new bureaucratic task. "Okay," he says wondering how he's going to break the news to his wife and stay alive long enough to go to court.

Monica

The day began as it always did for Monica. She woke up at 6:30 to a snoring husband and quietly got out of bed. Tiptoeing across the dark room, she grabbed her bathrobe and closed the door, stepping into the hall and turning on the light. She was never truly awake until the first coffee. Two children aged three and six meant having a relaxing cup first thing in the morning was a tradition of the past like late nights out with girlfriends. The first thing she did now was check in on her sleeping angels, prepare their breakfast and then shower. The coffee would have to come a few hours later.

After a quick ten minute rinse, she walked into her bedroom and switched on the light, beginning stage two of the morning – waking the husband and getting dressed.

"*Cariño.* It's time to get up," she said going to the closet to pick out that day's outfit. Shifting through the clothes separated by article crammed in her small closet, she struggled to find something to wear, having already worn everything twice that month. Once upon a time she loved going shopping, but she hadn't bought any new clothes since last year's sales, another tradition of the past gone. The only thing more frustrating than not finding something to wear was the sound of her still snoring husband. She stopped searching, went to the bed, and rocked his limp body back and forth. "Come on, Juan, I have to get the kids up now."

He snorted, rolled onto his side and wrapped himself up tighter in the blanket.

She stopped shaking him and stamped her foot. "Juan! I'm starting to get angry."

"Okay, okay, just five more minutes," he grumbled. It was the same struggle every morning and she wondered if other women had to put up with husbands like this as she went to the closet, picked out the first matching skirt and blouse she saw and finished getting dressed.

The sound of running water meant Juan was in the shower. He did listen, she thought, smiling as she led her groggy children into the dining area off the living room for their breakfast and stage three of the day. She sat Juanito at the table and put Alba in the high-chair. In front of both were glasses of poured juice, prepared bowls of cereal and plates with fruit that she had cut into the shape of animals. "Mommy, I don't like this." It was her three year old daughter.

"Alba, *cariño*, you have to eat it to be big and strong." She walked up to the high-chair and lifted a spoon.

"I don't like it!" screamed the girl with a set of lungs of a future opera singer as she swung her arm, sending the bowl, plate and glass crashing to the ground, spraying Monica with milk, fruit and juice in the process.

"Alba!" she yelled before taking a deep breath, "*Cariño,* please eat your food."

The little girl had her mother's big, brown eyes and they narrowed in a familiar scowl as she pointed her chubby finger at the box of sugar puffs on the table by her brother. "I don't like this cereal! I want that!"

"You can't eat those! You'll get fat!" The puzzled look on her daughter's meant Alba didn't quite understand and Monica breathed a sigh of relief. She didn't mean for it to come out like that. She thought about what her mother had said the other week about trying to be more patient. "Do you want mommy to make you a fruit shake instead of cereal?"

"No!"

"Alba, *por favor.*"

"Nooo!"

"Alba!"

"*Hola cariño.* The kids almost ready?" Juan said entering the kitchen, straightening his tie. "I'm meeting some guys from work for breakfast, so I need to take off a little early."

She whipped her head around and offered her angriest stare. "Finish getting them dressed and make sure Alba wears a skirt and not pants. I need to put my make-up on and find a new outfit."

"But, c*ariño...*"

"Juan, I do everything around here. Can't you just do this *one* thing?"

She took his silence and guilty expression as a yes and went to the bathroom. Her husband's towel and pajamas were on the wet floor. She bit her lip to stop from slamming the door. Her reflection in the mirror told her what she had already known - she needed a vacation.

***

The metal elevator opened and Monica stepped out to the lobby of the apartment building for the start of stage four – the commute. In a few months she was to turn the dreaded forty, but she still tried to keep up with the latest fashion. Knee-length pencil skirts, leather boots and tight-fitting sweaters were all the rage that winter and she managed to pull off the ensemble, thanks to a svelte body that came from minimal eating. The *portera* had arrived early and sat at a desk with a newspaper. "Good morning, beautiful," said the silver-haired woman. "I just saw your husband and kids."

"*Hola*, Carmen. How's everything?"

"Good. There's a new couple in the building."

"Really?"

"Yes, *guiris*."

"Where from?"

"*Nordicos*, Swedish, Norwegian, Danish, I can't tell the difference. They're both tall, blond and blue-eyed."

"I went to Norway once. It's beautiful," Monica said, recalling the second vacation she and Juan took together.

"It's too cold for me there."

"Not in summer."

"I suppose so. Still, why leave Spain? It's the best. We have everything here."

"I didn't mean to live."

"Yes. I know." The old lady took off and wiped her glasses. "So, off to work?"

"Unfortunately." Monica glanced at her watch; the time was 7:55. "Alright, listen, as always, I'm running late, so I must go."

"Okay. Have a good day and kiss that adorable daughter of yours for me. She looked so cute in that skirt."

***

The rain from the previous night's storm left the ground wet and a light drizzle still fell from the charcoal sky. Opening her umbrella, Monica regretted choosing the new pointed-toe boots with heels as she gingerly stumbled down the slippery sidewalk towards the metro. The street lamps dimmed, indicating the start of a new day. As she passed a bright bakery, she smelled the fresh pastries and felt a craving for a hot ham and cheese croissant. She didn't have time to stop or to go back and change her shoes. She never seemed to have time anymore.

The metro was packed with rush hour commuters and standing room only. Getting on, Monica spotted a student preparing for the next stop and pushed through the businessmen in suits, the old women with their grandchildren and construction workers in blue overalls to claim the seat. A woman with a double chin had also seen the potential chance to sit and made her move. The student stood and eased her way towards the door. The two candidates went for the prize. Monica was a bit quicker and sat down, seeing off her defeated opponent with a victorious grin. A man in a suit sat next to her and read a free newspaper. The bold headline said: *La Crisis Afecta a España más que al Resto de Europa.* Below it a picture of *El Raval* vigilante that high-lighted the lead local story. It seemed it was only bad news or stories about crazies lately, Monica thought.

The man got up and left the paper on the seat. Like two people going for the last dinner roll, the teenage boy on the other side of him and Monica went for it. Again, she was just a bit quicker and after smiling at the boy in victory, she read the entertainment section on the back where headlines discussed the latest Hollywood stars and the lives of football players' wives. Flipping through it, she stopped at a special insert dedicated to the new luxury apartments for sale near the beach in Diagonal Mar. They were so modern and new compared to her flat. An apartment like those would be the first thing she bought when she won *la lotería,* she decided and turned to another section. Color photos of packaged vacations were splashed on the page and she day-dreamed of visiting China or Thailand. At first she imagined going alone. Then she thought, how boring, and pictured a chiseled, blue eyed young man for a little fun. It only lasted a couple of seconds before she thought of her husband and kids.

Her office was located in a tall, copper-colored building near Plaça Espanya. Walking into the lobby, she had her daily chat with the security guard, went through the finger-print scanning turnstiles and got in a waiting elevator. Most of her coworkers arrived between nine and ten. She liked getting there a half hour early, not to work, but for stage five – her first cup of coffee.

Two years ago, when economic times had been good, the company splurged on an espresso machine for the employees. The strong aroma of an Italian blend began to awaken her sleepy senses, making her feel like a model in a gourmet coffee commercial. Sipping on the plastic cup, she looked out the window of the break room to the tenth floor patio. The sky was full of ominous black clouds, but the drizzle had stopped. The human resources director stood by the railing, smoking and gazing onto the yellow cranes spanning the Barcelona sky line. Her good looks and young age made Elena a frequent topic of office gossip, but Monica had always gotten along with her.

"*Buenos dias,*" Monica said waking out into the chilly damp air. "Why are you out here? It's freezing."

Elena seemed startled by the question. "Oh, *Buenos dias,* Monica. How are things?"

"I'm tired."

"Me, too. I didn't get home until nine last night. My husband wasn't too pleased."

Monica laughed. "He sounds like me when it comes to Juan."

"Does he come home late a lot?"

"Sometimes, usually when the kid's have been acting up."

Elena smiled. "And how are your little angels?"

Monica described the morning.

"Oh."

"Do you have kids?"

"Two teenage step-sons. They just think about girls and football."

"I'm not looking forward to my children becoming teenagers. They're a handful as it is, especially my daughter. She's a monster."

"Being the step-mom, I usually let their father do most of the work and stay out of complicated issues." Elena stomped out her cigarette. "Alright, I must go to a meeting now."

"Okay. See you around, Elena."

"See you around, Monica. Have a good day."

***

Stage six saw Monica at her desk and ready to work at nine o'clock every morning Monday through Friday. The caffeine had kicked in and for the first time that day, she could say she was awake. Her inbox was full of emails, most coming from the multinational's headquarters in Germany. She was the assistant to the finance director. He hadn't arrived yet, but there was a new stack of papers on the desk detailing her daily tasks. She had to prepare a two hour presentation for tomorrow's steering committee meeting. The same one she had scheduled it on his agenda three weeks ago. Everything was always last minute and urgent with him as it was with every other boss from whom she had worked.

Picking up the pile, she thumbed through the loose papers to get an idea of the task. Her boss had been with the company since it opened its Spanish office and using a computer wasn't his strong suit. On sheets of paper torn from a notebook were scribbled drawings of slides he wanted, along with hand-written notes pointing to the department to contact for the relevant information. Monica set down the papers and opened up Power Point.

***

"Do you want to grab breakfast?" It was the sale manager's assistant, Mar. The digital clock on the desk read 11:20 a.m.

"Sure," Monica said. About half the slides had been completed, but she still didn't have any of the requested figures. "By the way, Mar, do you think you could e-mail last quarter's sales and costs before we go?"

There was a second's pause and Monica wondered if her coworker had checked her email or voice-box yet.

"Um, can I do it when we come back? I promise it'll be the first thing I do. I'm starving right now and need to eat."

"Fine, but first thing. It's for the big bosses in Germany."

"Yes, I know. I promise as soon as we get back."

The office bar was just around the corner and full of coworkers eating, smoking and drinking coffee. Walking to the far back away from everyone, the two assistants sat at a small round table on some short stools. As they waited to be served, Mar asked, "Did you hear the rumors?"

"No, what?" replied Monica.

"Germany's ordered staff reductions."

"How do you know?"

"I overheard Elena and the general manager talking on the patio."

"Wow."

"How long have you been here?"

"Fifteen years."

"You'll get a nice severance package then."

"I guess, but we couldn't afford to lose my income."
Monica's mobile phone on the table flashed and the
ring-tone for the song "I'm Walking on Sunshine" began
to play. The name on the display was Manel, her boss.
"*Si,*" she said.

"Where are you?"

"Having breakfast."

"Did you see my note?"

"Yes, I'm making progress. I'm just waiting for people
to get back to me."

"Very good. You also need to translate it into English
and send it to Germany by five."

"I'll try."

"They have to receive it by the end of the day. They
were supposed to have gotten it three days ago."

"Can you call the other departments and tell them to
send me the info?"

"No. I have a meeting with a client right now and I'm
not at the office."

"Okay." Monica hung up. The waiter arrived and she
ordered a ham and cheese croissant and fresh squeezed
orange juice. She took her time eating and either
gossiping or complaining about coworkers, celebrities
and family. And when she was finished eating, she
enjoyed a second cup of coffee making breakfast her
favorite stage of the day.

***

Monica had done all of the layout and design of the
presentation in Spanish and translated most of it into
English by the time lunch, or stage eight, arrived. Of the
required information, Mar had sent the figures for the
sales department and Rosa, the numbers for logistics. She
still waited on the usual suspects: marketing, HR, and IT.

She picked up the phone to see what the holdup was. The melody for "I'm Walking on Sunshine" began to play and she set down the receiver. She looked at her flashing mobile; it was the school's number. "*Si?*"

"Monica?"

"*Si.*"

"*Hola,* I'm calling from the nurse's office. Your son's been throwing up and started running a fever."

The image of an ill and helpless son flashed making Monica feel sick with worry. "Oh, no! My poor baby."

"He should probably go home. When can you pick him up?"

"I'm at work now and I don't think I can leave. Let me call my mother."

She hung up and pressed one, speed-dialing her parent's home.

"*Mamá.*"

"*Si?*"

"Juanito's ill. Can you pick him up from school and watch him? I'll try to leave work early."

"I'm very sorry, but don't you remember? Your father's scheduled for cataract surgery this afternoon. We're just on our way out the door."

Monica had forgotten. "Of course, that's right. Give him a kiss for me."

"What are you going to do? Can Maria do it?"

"No, she and Juan Senior are at their home on Menorca. They won't be back until next week."

"And Juan?"

"I'm going to call him right now and see."

"Okay. If not, I could do it while your father's in surgery. I'd have to bring Juanito to the hospital, though."

"No, don't worry about it. Take care of *papá.* I'll call you tonight." She hung up and pushed two for speed-dial. Her husband's phone rang and cut to voice-mail. She left a message and closed her eyes to stop from crying. This was the last thing she needed.

The only personal item the desk was a framed photo of her and the children from last summer at her parents-in-law's beach house. It was the first image Monica saw, not that her decision required much thinking. It was breaking the news to her boss that was the hard part. Standing up, she sniffed and walked to a glass walled office. The door was closed and Manel sat with his feet up, talking on the phone. She knocked. He straightened, hung up and waved her in. "Yes."

She explained the situation.

"Monica, you've seen the work we've got today. Normally, I don't mind you leaving a little early. But, not before lunch!"

"Yes, I know, Manel. The only thing left is getting the numbers and maybe Mar could do it."

"Mar! She doesn't know her head from her ass. Everything is impossible and a struggle with her." He motioned for Monica to sit down. "If I still wanted her as an assistant, she would be. But she isn't. Do you know why?"

"No," she said taking a seat.

"Because Elena said you were the most competent and professional one here."

"Really?" He had never complimented her before.

"Yes, and I thought so too. Now, I'm not so sure."

"I know it's not a good day. But it's an emergency."

The hard look in his eyes conveyed little sympathy.

"Have you finished translating it?"

"Almost. I thought Johnny might be able to do it. It would sound much better."

"Who?"

"Your English teacher."

He paused and mulled. "You saw in the presentation that the Germans are ordering staff-reductions?"

"Yes." She thought about how to respond to such a blanket threat and used her knowledge of Spanish labor laws from her time studying to be a state employee to call his bluff. "I also know the cost of laying me off will cost nearly two years in salary." She paused to check his expression: surprised with an amused grin. She used her knowledge of office gossip for the closer. "Besides, you've gone through every assistant and I'm the only one who'll put up with you."

Her boss coughed, "Is that so?"

Monica couldn't tell if he was ready to explode or in a state of shock. She didn't think he knew either. She stood up. This topic was no longer up for discussion. Her son needed her and she had to leave. "So, I'll tell Mar to get the figures and call Johnny. I'll also try to come in a bit early tomorrow."

"Um, okay." Like most men, all it took was a firm woman to turn Manel into a baby lamb.

***

On a nearly empty metro car, the courage and confidence Monica had felt in her boss's office left at the sight of the headline of one of the main dailies laying on an empty seat. *La Crisis* was written in big bold letters with a list of companies and factories laying off workers and a flashy graph showing unemployment rising to twenty-percent. It seemed no one was safe. She started looking at the phone in her hands, expecting a call from Elena and human resources saying she was fired. It stayed silent. Going up the escalators, a gray sky continued to cast a gloom over the city and isolated drops of rain pelted the concrete. She opened the umbrella and started walking. A few streets down, the smooth sole of her boot slipped on the wet pavement. "*Coño – ¡Me cago en dios y su puta madre!*" she shouted loud enough for someone on Tibidabo Mountain to hear, as her still firm backside bounced off the hard cement.

A group of construction workers rushed out of a bar. "You okay, beautiful?" they asked spitting crumbs and helping her to the feet.

She wiped the back of her soaked skirt and sore derrière and replied, "Just a little embarrassed," as a twinge of pain ran down her legs.

The youngest of the group put his arm around her. "You single, *guapa*?"

"You picking me up?" She stepped away and smiled. He was cute in that bad boy kind of way with piercings and tattoos, but really not her type - she liked the more professional and clean look.

"It's not every day I get to help out a beautiful woman."

"I'm a little old for you." She teasingly pinched his cheek.

"I like mature women," he shouted as she carefully, and painfully, sashayed down the street. After all, it wasn't every day she got two compliments.

***

The school was run by a Franciscan order of nuns, who oversaw the daycare for her three year old daughter, the primary education for her five year old son, and the after-school service for the both on them until five o'clock, at which point her mother usually picked them up and babysat until six or seven. The thought of Juan ill and alone filled Monica with a painful urgency that dulled the pain from the fall as she hurried down the school corridor to the rapid clicks of her heels hitting the linoleum floor.

She entered an empty nurse's office and ran up to the desk. She banged a bell. No one came. She leaned over and saw Juanito slumped in a chair in a corner by the toilet. Lifting the table top to pass, she sprinted to him. "*Mi pobrecito niño.* Are you okay?" she said, holding him tight, running her fingers through his clammy hair.

"Are you taking me home, mommy?"

She touched a burning forehead. "Of course, I am. And I'm going to take good care of you."

The door opened and the nurse came in from the corridor. "He'll probably need to stay at home a few days."

"Okay. Thank you," Monica replied as she lifted her sick son so his head rested on her shoulder and carried him out. She made it halfway down to the corridor before her throbbing back, legs and arms made carrying Juanito impossible and she set him down. A door to a classroom was open a crack and she saw Alba standing near a crying girl with a toy in hand. Sitting Juanito down on a chair by a water fountain, she looked into his cloudy eyes. "Wait for mommy, *vale*? I'll be right back."

He moaned in confirmation.

By the time she got to the door, the teacher was now having a serious word with her daughter who still clenched the toy. Monica knocked. The young girl stopped, sat Alba down in a chair facing the wall, and came to the door. "Yes," she said trying to mask her frustration.

"I'm Alba's mother."

"Oh." She studied Monica intently.

"Is she doing anything important today?"

"No."

"Can I take her from class?"

The girl's face lit up and she said, "By all means," before turning to a room of screaming toddlers and shouting, "Alba!"

The little girl sat up and turned around. Her big brown eyes widened and the look of joyous surprise on her face eased the pain in Monica's backside, arms and back. "*¡Mamá!*" she cried, throwing down the toy as she ran towards her mother's outstretched arms.

Filled with a newfound strength, Monica lifted her daughter and repeatedly kissed her chubby cheek. "*Hola mi niña*. Have you missed me?"

Alba pushed off her mother's shoulder and looked at her suspiciously. "Why are you here? Am I in trouble again?"

"No, no. Your brother, you and I and going to spend the afternoon together."

"At home? Can I watch *Los Lunis*?"

"Of course."

"Yeeeaaaah!"

***

The few drops had turned into a steady shower by the time Monica and her two children left the school and walked down the stone steps. Gathering them in close, she opened the umbrella and they headed down the path towards the traffic racing and splashing down Carrer Balmes. Alba pointed to her mother's limp. "What's wrong mommy?"

"Mommy had a little accident."

"Are you hurt?" asked her son.

"No, I'm okay. Come on. Let's get a taxi."

"I thought *papá* said no more taxis." Monica's three-year reminded her.

"*Papá's* not here, is he?"

109

She hailed a cab and ushered her children in the back seat. Giving the driver the address, she sat back and relaxed for the first time that day. Her sick son's head lay on her lap and her daughter kept busy drawing smiley faces in the condensation on the window. "I'm Walking on Sunshine" began to play on her mobile and she saw her husband's name flashing. He always knew just *not* when to call.

"*Hola cariño.*" His tone was contrite. "Sorry, I was stuck in a three-hour meeting. You know how it is. How's Juanito?"

"Sick."

"Who ended up picking him up?"

"I did."

"How'd Manel take it?"

"I'm not sure, to tell you the truth. We'll see if I have a job tomorrow."

"Oh." He paused for a good two seconds. "By the way, I've got some good news."

"What?"

"Mom and Dad said we can use their house on Menorca for the Easter holidays."

"The water's too cold to go swimming then."

"I know. But I thought it'd be nice to get out of Barcelona."

"We'll see."

"Um, okay. Let me know. You okay?"

"No, I fell and I'm in pain. Look Juan, I'll see you tonight, okay?"

"Um, okay. I'll try and leave work early. A big client's just cut the budget, so every one's running around and stressed out."

"Okay."

Monica hung up the phone. He said the same thing every time there was an emergency and she had to take off work. She only remembered him coming through five times in ten years of marriage. There was the week after she had an emergency appendectomy and the days when she almost miscarried with Alba. There was also the two weeks following the birth of each of their two children and the day after her favorite uncle died. That was it. Then again, Mar's husband missed the birth of the only child while on a fishing trip and was incapable of putting a dish in the dishwasher. Like everything in life, husbands were relative, she decided.

***

Back at home and in the kitchen, Monica popped two ibuprofens for her now stiffening back and washed them down with a glass of water. "I'm Walking on Sunshine" began to play again and she looked down on the counter to her flashing phone. It was her office. "*Si*."

"*Hola* Monica. It's Elena. How are you?"

"I'm fine. Juanito's sick, though."

"Yes, I heard. Is it serious?"

"I think it's just the flu. I'm taking him to the doctor tomorrow morning."

"Are you coming to work after?"

It had been such a hectic day that Monica hadn't given tomorrow much thought yet. Her father had outpatient surgery, which meant she could leave Juanito with her parents, like she always did in these situations. Plus, Manel needed her. He was a gruff and demanding boss, but he had always been fair and understanding. Now Germany had a new, young regional head. Monica had been around long enough to know when there was a new chief, somebody had to be sacrificed and an antiquated boss made the perfect person. She readied to tell Elena *Yes*.

A handmade Christmas card on the refrigerator gave her pause. Using brown cardboard as the base, green paper crudely cut into the shape of leafs and red beads for berries as the frame, its centerpiece was a photo of Juanito and her after a violin recital. Her husband thought it was a bit on the sensitive side, but to Monica, it was better than the gold necklace he had bought her.

"I don't think so, Elena." She explained the situation with her parents and the need to take care of a sick son.

There was a moment of hesitation at the answer. "Um, okay, Monica. No problem. I understand."

"Will I still have a job?"

Elena laughed. "Of course you will. Manel will be upset, but I know how to handle him. I'll have Mar help out and Ana at reception."

"Thanks, Elena."

"Don't worry. Just make sure to bring a copy of the doctor's note and dock the days from your vacation time."

"Okay. I'll let you know something tomorrow."

"Sounds good." Monica hung up the phone. In the upper corner of the screen an icon of an envelope told her she had a message. *How about Disney Land Paris for Easter? Claudia can watch the kids and we'll spend a weekend in the city? Juan.*

She was touched by the attempt. Her husband was good at the small things and spoiled her and the kids. The thought of her children with her twenty-five year old sister-in-law made the offer a nonstarter, however. She texted back her preference for a quiet weekend at home with maybe a dinner and a movie out. He responded *sure* in under a minute.

On the counter was a tray with the sugar puffs, a carton of orange juice and two sets of glasses, bowls and spoons. Monica picked it up and walked out to a hall. There was no screaming, banging, or water running. She couldn't remember the last time the house had been so quiet. She stood there for a minute and enjoyed it like her birthday ten years ago at the Palau de Musica, letting the symphony of silence take her away to a tropical island as if it were a classical orchestra. Today was turning into one of those rare good days. And like the calm in the house, she couldn't remember the last time she had one of those.

Carrying the tray into the bedroom, she found Juanito curled up and hugging a pillow on one side and Alba watching her favorite cartoon on the flat-screen across the room on the other. Her eyes drooped and Monica knew it was just a question of time before the little monster was sound asleep. She smiled, set down the tray and turned off the TV. Crawling into the space between her two children, she brought them in close and closed her eyes. The patter of their heart beats mixed with the falling rain to sooth and relax her mind and body, expunging all the daily worries and concerns from her thoughts as drowsiness set in like a creeping bank of fog and Monica slept her first siesta in years.

Running the Gauntlet

At the bottom of the Barrio Gotico was the dark and dusty Carrer Ample. Meaning "wide street" in Catalan, it stretched from las Ramblas to Via Laietana and had been the last main road of the medieval walled city, where black-smiths, shoe-makers and tailors applied their trades on the ground floor of the stone buildings. The wall that once surrounded Barcelona had long since been torn down and replaced by the boulevard Passeig d'Isabel II at end of the nineteenth century. The buildings made of centuries old stone and mortar remained, however, and nowadays, convenience stores, fusion restaurants and kitsch bars lined each side of the street just slightly wider than an alley, making it a popular destination for those looking to party.

Four men met at one such watering hole called Hook. A small, dark bar with wood paneling, its decorative inspiration came, as its name implied, from the famous pirate Captain Hook of *Peter Pan* whose wooden statue guarded the front door. Inside peg legs hung from the ceiling, eye patches adorned the walls as bartenders clad in puffy white shirts served drinks to mostly tourists and expats in t-shirts and shorts. At the corner by the window near an old sea chest, the four men sat around a table and discussed that night's plan.

"Right," the first man, George, said in the tone and intonation of an English gentleman. "I'm glad to see the three of you are here."

"*Sss*...What about *Mahk*, Dan and *Olivah*?" The words were spoken with a whistle and a strong New England accent that dropped the 'R' from many words.

George stared at the bruised baby face and split lip of the second man, Tommy, whose unruly curly blond hair looked like a greasy afro. "They are obviously cowards. And would you wash your hair. You might be from Africa, but you don't have to look like Tarzan."

"They say it washes itself after six months." Tommy stuck a rolled cigarette in his mouth and lit it. "But you don't have to worry about that, do you?"

Taking a handkerchief from his pressed shirt pocket, George dabbed the sweat beading on his forehead and brushed back the few long stands on top of his head. "Baldness is hereditary. I have no control over it. You, on the other hand, do have control over looking like a civilized human being. Had your parents sent you to a proper boarding school in the UK and not in Boston, you would've known that."

A high pitched voice lisped, "Is Sam coming?"

"I've already told you, Paco, *His phone's off.*" He neatly folded handkerchief and put it back in his shirt's breast pocket as he glared at the third member of the group - a short, Spaniard with a shaved head and bulging eyes which made him look like a character in *The Simpsons*. "So, please stop asking."

He next turned to a pock-marked blond boy with a new Louis Vuitton hat cocked to the side. "Have you spoken to Jared and his crew?"

"*Yez*, he is busy *takeen* care of *sometheen* at the *Poart* and cannot come," said the fourth and final member, Morgan from France.

"Then it'll just be the fou' of us?" Tommy asked with a rising intonation as if the answer made a difference.

115

"That seems to be the case." George stood to address the men. He was a tall, thin man who liked to wear his button down shirts tucked into hiked trousers and had the small mustache above his lip popular during the Great British empire. "I'd rather have four men committed to the cause than an army of a hundred mercenaries." He clapped and rubbed his hands together. "Right, who wants a drink then? My shout."

The men raised their hands. He picked Paco to help with the order and went to the bar. They came back with four tube glasses three quarters full of Cuban rum over three ice cubes and four small coke bottles.

George poured some of the coke in the glass, stirred and licked his finger. "I guess they attacked someone again. One of my teachers near the Marsella."

Touching the fresh scab on his lip with his tongue and feeling where a front tooth once was, Tommy replied, "They're such fuckers."

"They" were the dark forces that seemed to run Barcelona's old city at night. Bands of shady men who belonged to shadowy mafias, they pimped the street hookers and sold bad quality drugs. Their most infamous source of income, however, came from robbing tourists and expats looking for a good time at the hundreds of bars and clubs hidden in the labyrinth of cobblestone alleys of *El Barrio Gotico* and *El Raval*. And while those two neighborhoods had always had a reputation for such petty crime, like the establishments in their centuries old ground floors, the nature and frequency of the attacks were changing.

The only Spaniard of the group, Paco asked, "Did you read the article in *La Vanguardia* last week?"

"No. I don't read the Spanish press," replied George crunching on a melted ice cube.

"They say the rise in crime and violence is the tourists' fault for getting so drunk."

"Is that so?" He chewed on the parts of the ice and swallowed. "Look, I'm not proud of my British brethren who come here, but that's a bit much to put it all on us."

"What? I don't understand."

"What I'm saying is," he licked his lips, "everyone knows there's a deal between the police and the mafias. As long as they don't target the Spanish and pay the bribes, the Old Bill looks the other way."

"But I'm *Espanish*."

"The Catalans then."

Paco slurped his drink. "I don't know."

"He'sss right," Tommy whistled through his missing front tooth. "After they got me, I went to a bar and the owner said that's why they never report anything. It'd make no difference and piss off the mafias."

"But that's what the paper said!"

George looked at the small Spaniard with the cold hard stare his father used when he made a stupid comment as a child and gave him the same silent response. Reaching under his seat, he lifted a half-empty duffel bag and laid it down on the round table. "Right. I've made us all t-shirts," he said, unzipping it, pulling out a black shirt for each of them.

Morgan held it up to his XXL paisley polo. *Taking the Streets Back* in big white letters was printed on the front. "Why do we need these?"

"So, when the press and the police ask them who did it, this sentence will be what they report." He zipped up the bag.

"What *happenz* if they do not speak English?"

George's dumbfounded expression revealed that he hadn't thought of that possibility. "I'm sure one of them will," he replied as he slung the duffel bag over his shoulder to the racket of sliding and banging cans. "Right, men. Time to get a move on. We'll put the shirts on right before we run the gauntlet, so as not to attract too much attention along the way."

***

Carrer Ample was alive with revelers staggering in and out of the many bars on their way to their next stop. At the bright light of a late night convenience store, a group of Americans stumbled out, shouting, "This place fuckin' rocks, man," with tall cans of beer in hand. A few doors down was a sign with the roman letters of a trade that had survived the changes of time, a Spanish shoe store. A blond student sat in front of its closed metal shutter with her arms wrapped around her knees, her head buried in her lap.

George heard the click of a camera phone and looked down at Paco. "What on bloody earth are you doing?"

"I like taking pictures of beautiful women."

"But she's fucking smashed."

"She's still pretty."

Morgan laughed. "Aren't you gay?"

Paco's bulging eyes popped out of his round head like a *Looney Tunes* cartoon character. "No! I love women. Look! All these pictures."

He showed his phone to Morgan and flipped through photo after photo of different, unsuspecting girls.

"Who *iz* that?"

"Who's this?" Paco stopped at one with long strawberry hair. "This is my flat mate."

George had heard enough and pushed Paco to the side. "Get away from this woman, you sick bastard."

"What? I don't understand. I like taking pictures."

He paid him no mind and bent down to aid the drunk student. "Miss, are you alright? This isn't a good place to be in this state," he said giving her a hard tap on the shoulder. "Where do you live?"

"Grgh."

"Miss, miss." It took him a few minutes of shaking the girl so hard her head whipped to sober her up enough to find out an address. Hailing a taxi that drove down the one way street, he put her in back, gave the driver a twenty and sent her on the way. He turned around to see Paco and Morgan. "Where's Tommy?"

"He had to go to the *bathrooom*," replied the Frenchman flicking his smoke into the street.

"For fuck's sake. Hold this." He handed Morgan the duffel bag and went back to Hook for the second member of the group.

***

Looking over the heads of the crowd in the dark wooden bar, George saw Tommy's greasy blond afro poking up by a pirate statue in the far back corner. He impatiently pushed through the crowd and discovered his friend talking to three tall blonds. "Tommy!"

"Hey, George." The boy had a fresh drink in hand and beamed a gap toothed smile. "May I present to you - Ingrid, Olga and Kirstin? They're from Sweden."

"Allo!" the three girls said cheerily.

He was not impressed and yanked his friend's arm, pulling him to the side. "What are you doing? I said we had to get a move on."

Tommy kicked the floor. "Yeah, I know. It's just that..."

"That what?"

"I dunno. There's only four of us and, I dunno, I just don't think tonight is a good idea anymore."

"Is that so?"

"Yeah."

"How many times have you been robbed?" George brought up the four muggings Tommy had suffered in his year in Barcelona and the two times he ended up in the hospital as a result. He also reminded his young friend of the fact that he swore after the last time he'd get his revenge. "Now," he said with authority, "I know you're only twenty-one, but there comes a time in every man's life when he must either stand up and fight or shut up and stop complaining. What are you gonna do?"

"I dunno, man." Tommy set his drink on a table and pulled out his pouch of tobacco. "I'm only in Barcelona a few more months before I go back to Africa to work at my parents' hotel. I just wanna have fun, you know?"

"I see." He did little to disguise his disappointment in his tone or face. Tommy had been the first person to answer his ad in the Barcelona Connect looking for people who were "sick of being a victim to scum" as he put it. He was also the only one to come to the all five of the subsequent meetings, where George laid out his plan to take on the mafias that had mugged his favorite auntie and ruined her holiday. "Alright, then, I'm not going to beg. Good luck to you, Tommy," he said, turning on his heel and leaving without giving his friend a chance to answer.

***

Amid the teeming crowds on Carrer Ample, George found Paco and Morgan standing at the corner of one of the many alleys that ran off the street.

"Where's Tommy?" asked the Frenchman handing him the duffel bag.

George took it and secured it over his shoulder so it was tucked tightly under his arm. "He ate some bad seafood and isn't feeling well."

"He looked okay to me," lisped Paco.

George scolded him with a silent scowl and then looked to Morgan. "Right, let's get a move on."

"I 'ave to meet some people at Bar Tequila."

"For fuck's sake! I thought we all agreed to treat tonight seriously." He looked down the street from where he had just come. "Now Tommy's dropped out and you've gone and made plans."

Morgan strolled over to him and put a hand on the English man's shoulder. "Relax man. It'll be quick and it's on the way."

"That's not the point!" He ranted how for close to two months they had been planning this evening and after each meeting, he had given them each a chance to back out, only for everyone to promise that they were as committed as him. "I need to know I can count on you. Because if not – fuck off. I'll do it myself."

A sly smile crept across Morgan's face. "You don't 'ave to worry about me, man. They got my little *sistur*." He took out a smoke and lit it. "And the last *motherfuckur* to hurt my *sistur*, I put in the 'ospital."

The small mustache above George's lip wrinkled as he grinned and put his arm around Morgan. "You know, Frenchie – I take back everything bad I ever said about you lot."

"I won't leave you either," added Paco looking up through his cartoonishly, big eyes.

George offered the rarest of sights from an English gentleman - a tooth showing smile. "Then it will be just us three musketeers," he said full of righteous and noble pride as he led his men up the dark alley and away from

Carrer Ample, through the maze of narrow and twisting streets to the muffled clangs of cans in the duffel bag and the stomps of marching feet.

***

Their trek ended at a medieval square with a modern sculpture of an orange ball on top of a twisting metal pole that rested in the middle of a raised concrete platform. Surrounding it were the metal tables of the many bars that populated the perimeter and watching it all was a camera on the wall next to a marble street sign that said *Plaça de George Orwell* in Roman letters.

George scanned the scene of the twenty-somethings drinking and smoking outside amid the begging junkies and their mangy dogs. The square made his stomach knot in disgust and he wondered what its famous namesake would have thought of such a place. "Where is this bar, Morgan?"

"You've never been to Bar Tequila? It's an institution."

"I try to avoid the city center."

Paco sashayed to the front and took the lead. "I know where it is!"

On the other side of the square was a bright red door with the word *Tequila* written in black slanted letters. Stepping through a padded door, they entered a dark place that stretched back like a mine shaft. Adorning its neon, blood-red walls were a collection of framed posters of 1980's heavy metal groups and the music of Metallica coming from the speakers above was so low, it seemed more appropriate for an elevator than a bar.

"What would you two like to drink?" George asked walking up to order from a scantily dressed female bartender.

"The usual, whiskey and coke," replied Morgan as he slipped on a pair of headphones which hung from the glass rack of the bar. The blasting music they piped through had him quickly putting them back.

Paco clapped his hands in excitement. "I want an apple martini!"

"Are you sure you're not gay?" George looked down at the man the size of a midget in a tight shirt and short denim shorts. "It's no big deal if you are. A relative in England recently came out."

"No! I love women!" Paco took out his phone to show the pictures of all the women he had snapped over the years to prove it.

"You know what, mate? You need to stop doing that. It's creepy," George turned to the bartender to order the drinks. "*Dos whiskeys y Coca-Cola y un apple mahtini, poh favoh,*" he said in Spanish with a thick English accent that made pronouncing the hard 'R' impossible.

The female bartender's face strained to understand the order. "Um, *Vale*"

Watching as the girl with enough piercings to qualify as a pin cushion made their drinks, George leaned in close to Morgan and whispered, "What a shame."

"What?"

"I don't understand why pretty girls feel the need to ruin their looks with piercings and tattoos."

Morgan laughed as the girl returned with the order. "You don't like them?"

"No."

"You've come to the wrong city then."

"I know." George paused and noticed Paco sitting on a stool with headphones, banging his head to the music of Iron Maiden that now played in the bar. "He's a strange one, isn't he?"

Morgan poured the coke into his glass and took a sip of his drink. "Very. How do you know him?"

"He's my wife's cousin."

"You're married?"

"Yes, to a wonderful Catalan woman with a beautiful daughter. Why else would I be here?"

The door opened and the shouting conversations from the street flooded the bar, blocking out the fading music. A group of three men entered. The door closed and a song by *Rage Against the Machine* now came softly from the speakers.

"*Bonsoir.*" They spoke in French.

As George sipped on his drink, he listened and watched Morgan and the three mean talk, but he didn't understand their conversation having not studied French for almost twenty years. A minute later, the men set down their half-drunk beers and slipped Morgan some money. In return, he gave them a small plastic bag of white powder. It was quick and discrete. "*Merci,*" they said and left the bar to a blast of noise from the street.

"You're a drug dealer?" George said.

"Shhh." Morgan put his finger to his lips. "Is there a problem?"

He looked at the hard, pock-marked face of the French man. "No, I suppose not."

"You don't do drugs?"

"No. I tried 'e' once in the nineties, but drugs aren't really my thing." He downed his drink. "I think I'm the only one in Barcelona who doesn't do them, though."

Morgan confirmed his suspicions with a knowing grin. "It sure seems that way, another drink?"

"Spot on." George looked past an elevated deejay booth to a back room of nothing but empty tables. "We should probably sit down and go over tonight's plan one last time."

"Okay. I'll meet you there."

***

"Rock you like a Hurricane" by the Scorpions provided the background music as the three men sat at the back by the toilets and George detailed the plan of attack. They were to hit the dark forces in *El Raval*. Recent posts in the various forums and blogs dedicated to Barcelona reported a particular street where the bands of robbers gathered and targeted the tourists.

"Are there any questions?" George said as he lifted up the duffel bag to the rattle of cans and set it down on the table.

"Yes," replied Paco sipping on his second apple martini. "I still don't understand how we're going to attack them. I have never been in a fight in my life."

George unzipped the bag and pulled out a can of hairspray. A kitchen lighter was taped to its front with its long nose directly under the can's nozzle, its igniter button sticking out for easy striking. He held out one for all to see. "With these."

Morgan smiled in appreciation at the contraption. "You are like Q from the James Bond films."

"Thank you. It was British ingenuity that drove the empire." He put the can back in the bag.

"But won't it burn them?" asked Paco.

"That's the idea." George finished his third and final drink of the night. "But hopefully they'll be smart enough to run once they smell their singed hair."

"I don't know. It seems a little crazy to me."

"Do you have any better ideas, Paco?"

"No."

George took a deep breath and said, "I know it's a bit extreme, but they have the numbers on their side." He contemplated what to say next. "And, while I abhor violence as much as the next man, desperate times call for desperate measures."

"Yes, I know, but this seems *really* crazy."

He dabbed his forehead with his handkerchief. "Paco, if we don't stand up to these men and put the fear of God into them, no one will."

"He's right," said Morgan. "They only understand violence."

Paco shook his head in disbelief. "Yes, yes, but we could go to jail!"

"Paco!" George snapped putting his handkerchief back. "How did you feel when these men held a knife to your throat and took all your money?"

"Violated and afraid."

"And what did you tell me the day after it happened?"

"That I was tired of always being the victim."

"Do you still feel that way?"

"Yes."

"Here's your chance to stop being the victim and show these cunts that their days of preying on the innocent are over!" George banged the table. "Now are you with us or not?"

"I suppose so. But what about the police?"

George snickered at the question. "Where were the police when Tommy was beaten, Morgan's little sister was mugged and my auntie was robbed?"

"I don't know."

"I'll tell you - in some restaurant having a coffee."

"You don't know that."

"Maybe not, but I do know they don't care about what's going on, because if they did, we wouldn't be here tonight." He stood up and brought the duffel bag close to his chest. The lights of the bar flashed on and off, indicating 2:30, closing time. "Right, men. The time is upon us," he said, his heart beating like a drum roll at the thought of some action.

***

Carrer Escudellers ran from Plaça De George Orwell to Las Ramblas. During the middle ages, it had been where potters spun clay into plates, cups and statues. Today ceramic knick-knack stores stood next to popular bars that fed booze to the tourists who stumbled onto centuries old streets to the rattle of closing shutters.

"We should probably wait until the crowd thins," whispered George as they walked out of Bar Tequila and onto the busy street. On the adjacent corner two police officers stood with guns at their side and observed young girls gather and debate where to go next. Their focus was so intense that they missed the three men pick the pocket of a kid in a baseball cap

"George," said Morgan smiling at the police's disinterest. "Can I ask you a question?"

"Sure."

"I know your favorite auntie was robbed, but why are you really doing this?"

"Well, Frenchie, because when I first arrived, they got me."

"How?"

"I was walking down the street by the Palau de Musica with my wife when a young boy fell off his bike." George explained how he rushed over to help the lad, only to have his pocket picked by two of the boy's friends as he bent down. He carried most of his cash and credit cards in a hidden money belt, so they didn't get much.

"But you see, they prey on the decency of men. And then, when they robbed my auntie and I saw Tommy's face, I just couldn't let it go anymore."

"I see." Morgan had on the black t-shirt with *Taking the Streets Back* in white letters over his paisley polo and George smiled for the second time that night. There were now only the isolated inebriated stragglers on the trash littered street and no more police presence. Setting off towards their final destination, they passed huddled groups of dark and shady characters lurking in the shadows on the corners of the crisscrossing alleys, chanting:

"Coke, marijuana, hashish, charlie."

"*Cerveza*, beer," chimed in a single man holding a plastic bag.

George turned to Morgan. "You seem like a bright chap. Have you ever thought about doing something else?"

Morgan grinned like he had heard that question before. "I am no different than the *bartendur*," he said waving at the closed metal shutters. "My clients are adults who can spend their money as they wish."

"Yes, I know, but booze is legal and drugs aren't."

Morgan laughed. "And what we are about to do is?"

"*Touché*," replied George as Carrer Escudellers came to an end near a waterless white fountain. Across the narrow one-way road flanking Las Ramblas street cleaners in green uniforms sprayed high powered hoses and strolled along side trucks with spinning brooms under their chassis. The blasting water acted like security guards at closing time, ushering all but the brave up the promenade towards the safety of Plaça Catalunya.

Within seconds, the first wave of prostitutes came to claim the territory. Staking out position under the lamps and near the closed newsstands, they were women from Africa and Eastern Europe whose toned muscles and hardened expressions revealed a toughness that provoked more fear than desire. And by the time the three men made it half way across the slippery promenade, a second wave of muscular transsexual hookers with bright wigs and fake breasts that resembled glued on volleyballs claimed the spaces by the closed animal stands.

Looking at the menacing girls and she-males blow kisses, George said, "Remember a few years ago when they were old, fat Spanish and Catalan women? Now, look at them."

"I think they're quiet pretty," replied Paco

George ignored his comment. They had reached the other side of the promenade and their final destination, Carrer de l'Arc del Teatre.

"This is it," he said quietly, watching as merry groups of party-goers passed under a white stone arch before meandering down an alley on their way to a knock-knock bar or after-hours club. It was a steady stream of men and women from their late teens to early thirties strolling under the lights of the street lamps on the buildings' walls. All appeared normal like it would have any other night. Then, without warning, the lights cut out and the white arch vanished into blackness amid the brightness of Las Ramblas.

Screams and cries rang through the air as if the street had now become the fun house from hell.

George shook with excitement at finally getting some vengeance on these filthy thieves, not for him, but for his favorite auntie, Tommy and anyone else whose holiday or time in Barcelona had been ruined by the scum. His pounding heart made it difficult to breathe and he struggled to say, "Ready to run the gauntlet, Frenchie."

"*Oui.*"

George looked for an answer from Paco but instead found him running away with one of the manly girls of the night, slamming the door of an available taxi. He faced a grinning Morgan. "And then, there were two."

"He was useless anyway."

The third smile of the night crossed George's face. "Remember, wait for my order."

Morgan nodded and they sprinted towards the desperate cries like firemen rushing into a burning home, entering the black hole that five seconds before had been a bright alley. The barks of men mixed with the flicks of lighters that spun heads in the darkness. Women's shrieks and men's shouts came from all directions as petrified cries for help hit ears in surround sound. It was impossible to tell who was who and where was where. George slowed to get his bearings. Two seconds later a hand reached deep in his pocket. It was a quick probe followed by a yelp that came with a handful of tacks. He pressed on the nozzle. "Now!"

Gas hissed. The lighter clicked. A flame whooshed. The would-be thief wailed in agony and fled with his hands covering his face. The alley was alight in the fiery orange of the spraying torch that made the black shadows on the walls dance like a medieval tribe around a bonfire. Both muggers and victims froze and looked at the crazed man with the blazing can in wide-eyed wonder – unsure if he was one of those fire jugglers common in Plaça Real or a demented criminal like "the Joker" from *Batman*. Screams of panic announced their decision.

A sudden gust of wind came from the maze of alleys, gathering strength and speed. Like a raging ghost who'd come to expel unwanted intruders, it howled and pushed the streaming torch back towards George's face. The flames grew closer and his right hand burned. He stopped pressing the lighter and let go. The alley was again dark. He heard the metal bounce off the stone ground and then a hiss followed by a booming explosion.

***

George slowly came to in a room at the Hospital del Mar with a view of the glistening sea and a stinging burn in his singed hands, arms and face. He was hooked up to drips and beeping machines and looking out of the bandages wrapped around his head, he saw the blurry outline of his wife sitting on a chair knitting.

His throat dry and scratched, he said in a raspy voice, "*Hola*, ducky. How long have I been out?"

"Two weeks," she replied in Catalan, her words bouncing around, echoing in his ringing head. She set down the needles and yarn, stood up and walked over to him. "How do you feel?"

"Like I've been grilled inside a church bell at noon." He spoke her native language, albeit with a thick English accent.

"George, this isn't a joke." She inspected the bandages that gave him the appearance of a mummy on Halloween and shook her head to stop from crying. "My God, George, what have you done? The police were just here."

"What did they say?"

"That you'll probably spend a few months in jail."

"I'm sorry, Nuria. I didn't think it'd go this far."

"What were you thinking?" She laid into him about the insanity of his dangerous and illegal actions and the price that she and their daughter had to pay. "For crying out loud, you're in all the papers and our neighbors think you're crazy!"

"I'm sorry, ducky. I really am." He looked into her tearing eyes and realized what a terrible mistake he had

131

made. His self-righteous desire to be the noble avenger had risked the only people who mattered and the sole reason he lived in this city - his family. "Please forgive me."

She went and looked out the window onto the sea. "I don't know, George."

"Do you know what happened to Morgan?"

"Who?"

"My French friend."

She whirled around and pointed an accusing finger. "The police say it was only you, George!"

"He didn't go through with it?" he whispered in shock at the realization. The thought of Morgan backing out under the cover of darkness stung worse than the sizzling burns and made the echoes in his ringing head pound like a jackhammer on a steel drum. As with Tommy, he had thought of Morgan as a new friend. He should have known better than to trust a drug dealer.

From Barcelona

The Crypt of Colonia Güell

1897

One of Barcelona's most famous architects found himself spending more and more time at his new studio. Located in the recently finished crypt of the Sagrada Familia, Antoni Gaudí had moved there to save on the cost of renting a work space and to take advantage of the sunlight that flooded through the windows placed high on the white stone walls. Providing him with enough natural light to work from sun-up to sun-set without the benefit of lamps or candles, the crypt's completion could not have come at a better time. The lack of donations for the church's continued construction meant he didn't have the money to spend on such frivolous expenses like lighting or rent for a studio. In fact, since he had taken on the commission fourteen years ago, he rarely had money for anything anymore. But he didn't care.

The Sagrada Familia wasn't meant for some wealthy industrialist or member of the Spanish royal family, but for a client with an endless amount of patience and whose reward would be greater than anything money could buy - the Lord Almighty. And, as such, it was to be the last great sanctuary of Christendom with eighteen soaring towers and three intricately carved façades that would trace the entire history of Christ from his birth to his death to his resurrection.

Building it had become an obsession. Visions came to him during the day or night, alone or with friends. More than mere flashes of inspiration, designs and ideas took shape in his mind like a jig-saw puzzle slowly coming together to form a vivid and clear picture. During these moments, his skin tingled and warmed as the Holy Spirit possessed him, filling him with a consuming fire to sketch until the Lord's designs were realized on thin cardboard, breaking the rapturous trance. Once finished with these drawings, he taped them to the walls of the studio to serve as a constant reminder of the perfection to which God made him aspire.

Of course, taking something sketched with charcoal pencils and turning it into a standing building fitting for the Christ the Lord was akin to building a castle on the Ebro delta just south of Barcelona – impossible given the amount of stone needed. The traditional method would have been to build a secondary wall and use flying buttresses to support the weight, but Gaudí saw that as a waste of space and too conventional for such a glorious edifice and client. Molding clay and plaster into scale models of his sketches, he played with the slopes and curves of the arches and columns, looking for ways to replicate the drawings in three dimensions, only to see the clay walls and towers sag and slump, indicating failure. He was literally being crushed by the weight of his designs.

Looking for guidance, he went to the Cathedral in *El Barrio Gotico* and prayed. Once again a vision came. This time, it wasn't a sketch he produced, but rather dangling chains of different lengths and attached sacks filled with lead pellets that hung from the ceiling of the studio which, depending on the time of day, glistened like palatial chandeliers.

***

A boy's high-pitched voice interrupted one such rapturous moment. Many things annoyed the architect – bourgeois opulence, Spanish who refuse to acknowledge *Catalunya* as different, over-friendly people – but nothing irritated him more than having his concentration broken, for it always happened just when everything was about to come together, resulting in a moment forever lost and impossible to reproduce.

"What?" he said standing on the top of a stool. He stopped stringing the chains and turned his head to see boy no older than thirteen in a black wool suit standing in the doorway to his studio.

"*Senyor* Güell requests your presence."

"*Senyor* Güell, you say?" The mention of his dear friend's name lightened Gaudí's mood and his angular face softened as he began to slowly climb down, wincing from the pain of his worn, arthritic bones rubbing together.

"Yes, sir. He's sent one of those new horseless coaches from Germany to fetch you."

"He did, did he?" He stroked his bushy blond beard and his blue eyes sparkled as he tried to picture the machine.

"Yes, sir. He's the first person in Barcelona to have one."

"Is that so? Well, let's see what *Senyor* Güell has spent his money on this time, shall we?" he said, taking a worn green coat from a rack by the door before he brushed past the boy and slowly ascended the stone steps that led outside.

***

It was a frigid, sunny January day. On the site of the future Sagrada Familia, mounds of uncut rock and stacks of stone slabs were piled high near empty benches and barrels. Abandoned scaffolding traced the perimeter of the barely laid fountain and hanging tarps flapped in the wind above shoulder-high walls. The boy's mouth opened to say something about the lack of workers, but stopped when he recalled *Senyor* Güell's warning not to mention the state of the church's construction. "So, what do you think of all the changes happening to Barcelona?" he said.

Staring at a semi-paved Carrer Mallorca and a ditch with a section of a lead sewage pipe set to be placed in it, Gaudí replied, "Welcome to the twentieth century."

"Yes, *Senyor* Güell says that there are now balloons that can take men across oceans!"

"Is that so?" Across the street was a new park with a pond and trees which Gaudí placed as sycamores. The thin branches sprouting from the trunks made them seem almost like skeletal arms capable of holding up the heavens and, staring at them, he thought back to the first time he saw such trees along Avenue des Champs-Elysées during the Paris World Fair almost twenty years ago.

***

He had been hired by the Comella Glove shop to design a case fitting for their most exclusive product. Using carved oak, forged iron and glass panes, he created a decorative display that seemed to be an extension of the jeweled glove, allowing for perfect viewing from all angles. Most of those in attendance at the fair looked at his creation with the bemused curiosity of an adult admiring the work of a precocious child and the glove failed to sell. But one wealthy Catalan industrialist named Eusebi Güell saw something much more and upon his return to Barcelona sought out Gaudí at his old studio. A devout Catholic like the architect, they discussed art, history and politics and by the end of the meeting, Gaudí received his first major commission.

137

***

"Sir? Sir?" The young boy tugged the architect's frayed coat sleeve bringing him back from the fond memory.

Gaudí squinted at the sycamores across the street in irritation. "Let's see if they've created a machine that can take us to Las Ramblas first, shall we?"

"Yes, sir. Follow me." The boy led him towards Carrer de Lepant where his curiosity was peaked at what appeared to be a steel horse-carriage with four wheels and no animal. He circled and inspected the contraption closely. Unlike something nature would create, it was totally symmetrical. The matching bicycle-like wheels were round with perfectly intertwined spokes; the only difference was the size, with the ones at the back being larger than the front. The polished black metal frame smoothly curved and bent on either side, holding a two person leather bench mounted on a vibrating wooden and metal trunk. In front was a straight brass pole with a wheel mounted on top like a sombrero and sitting behind it was a dark skinned Spaniard with a thick black mustache.

"What's your name?" Gaudí asked in Catalan.

"José, sir."

"Where you from?"

"Sevilla, sir."

Despite being fluent in *Castellano*, he did not change from his native language for any man, not even the King. He continued in Catalan, "Andaluz! What brings you to Barcelona?"

"Work, sir."

"Ah, yes, the pursuit of the all-mighty peseta. How do you find *Catalunya*?" A repetitive tap on the shoulder broke his train of thought evoking the seething annoyance of being interrupted for the third time. Wheeling around, he saw the trembling teenager holding a leather helmet, goggles and a scarf in out stretched arms.

"Sir, the journey can be very cold, so you'll need these."

The crow's feet around Gaudí's darkening blue eyes deepened as he prepared to deliver a scolding that was worse than any beating a priest at Catholic school could give. But when he looked at the boy's large eyes spread too far apart and a hook nose set to the left side of his head, he instead felt pity for the lad's misfortune of looking like a deformed lizard.

"What's your name?" he asked, his voice shaking with a barely contained rage.

"Jordi, sir."

"Jordi, has your father not told you to only speak when spoken to?"

"No, sir. My father died a few years ago."

The lines around Gaudí's misting eyes softened as he recalled his long dead mother whose passing continued to haunt him.

"Thank you, Jordi," he said taking the scarf and goggles. The young boy offered a wary smile and helped the architect up the steps and into the carriage before climbing in next to him without saying another word.

***

The construction boom currently underway in Barcelona meant some of the streets were paved with asphalt. Most of the roads of the L'Eixample district, however, remained loose gravel and the thin wheels of the horseless black carriage kicked up dirt, causing small pebbles to ricochet off the metal frame as it made its way towards Las Ramblas. People leading donkeys or pushing wheel barrows stopped and gawked at the sight of the strange machine barreling towards them in a cloud of dust. They quickly scattered at the blast of a horn when they realized it wasn't going to stop.

Riding on the open top of the roofless carriage turned Gaudí's exposed white cheeks a rosy shade of red as he looked through dusty goggles at a city transforming. Blue tarps hung from scaffolding and hid façades undergoing face-lifts, while steel frames provided the structure for new edifices to be erected. The pounding of hammers and chisels rang out like gunshots and the smoke of steamrollers rose in the air turning the blue sky brown. And despite the wind that now chapped his skin, he sat up in pride as he took in the sights and sounds, for those leading the city's renaissance weren't from Paris or Madrid, but fellow Catalans from the University of Superior Architectural Technique of Barcelona.

A bitter resentment began to seep in and sour his mood when he thought of his beloved Sagrada Familia sitting neglected, forgotten and behind schedule. Slumping in his seat, he cursed the materialistic leanings of the emerging bourgeoisie who would rather spend their newfound money turning their flats into palaces instead of on a magnificent House of God, without whom none of their wealth would be possible. Did they not understand, 'The Lord giveth and the Lord taketh away?' he thought, ruing the decline of true men of faith like him and Eusebi Güell.

Passing the glistening statuesque edifices that lined Las Ramblas and showcased the new Barcelona, the car turned right on tiny Nou de La Rambla and disappeared into the shadows of the medieval buildings of *El Raval*. Prostitutes, pimps and beggars crowded the dirty cobblestone street making progress slow as the driver honked and the black carriage pushed through the congestion. It finally stopped at two stone arches that framed black, wrought-iron gates, the wavy vertical bars of the main sections giving them the look of an Arabic mosaic with the initials "E" and "G" displayed in the middle of each. Above the black metal bars twisted like a slither of snakes and surrounded the five vertical stripes of the Catalan shield.

The gate opened and they drove into a courtyard to the smell of hay and horse manure rising from the open doors of the stables in the basement. The odor reminded Gaudí of his family's *masia* outside Reus where he spent much of his time alone wandering through the forest. The rattling engine cut and he watched Jordi quickly climb down from the carriage's top. "This is the first building you designed for *Senyor* Güell, isn't it?" the boy said, speaking the first words of the trip as he extended a hand to help the shivering architect.

Gaudí offered no reply as he carefully stepped down. Stoically looking up to the medieval style arched windows and black bars bent into a modern mazelike configurations, he said nothing about it being the work of a young architect and turned his attention to the street. People occasionally stopped and stared at the black iron eagle perched atop an iron cylinder between the wavy gates, most with a slack jawed expression of shock and horror, others simply snickered and pointed. He tried to dismiss them as uneducated and ignorant, but the sting of seeing his work mocked burned more than stepping on a wasps' nest. Turning away and walking to the palatial entrance, he left the boy still awaiting an answer to his question.

***

Eusebi Güell sat at a mahogany desk, reading a collection of poems and essays by his friend Joan Maragall. Set during medieval times in the Catalan countryside, the descriptions of forests, mountains and rivers were easy to picture and he caught himself laughing at the satirical tone of the unpolished prose. The influence of the Nietzsche in the vitality and symbolism of the words and themes was a bit too obvious for his liking, he being a devout man of God, and the German, the antichrist. But like the architectural revolution taking place outside his palace's walls, the tales of rural hardworking men who overcame an inhospitable nature to succeed were uniquely Catalan, filling him with nationalistic pride.

From one of Barcelona's wealthiest families, Güell had played a key role in the city's metamorphosis from Spain's forgotten second city into a modern European metropolis. Only a few years earlier speaking Catalan or displaying national symbols like the dragon or the bat meant jail time at the castle on Montjuïc Mountain. Now, thanks to the greater autonomy he and his fellow industrialists had negotiated with the King of Spain, those days were over, unleashing the great Catalan renaissance with the Güell name going down as Catalan Medici. Or, so he hoped.

Of course, when his friends learned of his affinity for the crazed architect Antoni Gaudí above all others, they laughed and ridiculed, citing the fantastical nature of his work and his prickly country temperament. Their pretentious derision cemented his faith in his friend. He might not have understood the art or the man, but as a student of history, Güell knew it was the original and the creative like Mozart who withstood the test of time and not the men like his main rival Salieri who could only reproduce the fashion of the moment – no matter how beautifully. A knock on the door stopped him from reading any further. "Come in," he said marking the page with a strip of velvet.

His young personal assistant, Jordi, entered. "*Senyor* Güell, Antoni Gaudí is here as requested."

"Fantastic. Send him in." He stood to greet his old friend.

The architect walked in with a warm smile. "Hello, Eusebi. It's been a long time," he said as the two embraced and kissed each other's cheeks.

"Yes, it has." Güell studied his old friend. "You look thin and tired, Antoni."

"As you've probably heard, donations for the Sagrada Familia have dried up for the time being."

"Yes, I'm sorry to hear that. You know, Antoni, when people pay for buildings, they don't expect sketches."

The architect's pale blue eyes turned black in anger. "Is it my fault Bocabella's original plan was flawed and a disservice to the Lord?"

"No, of course not." Güell laid a large hand adorned with jeweled rings on his friend's threadbare green jacket. "I'll call my accountant and see if we might be able to offer a donation to get things started."

Gaudí's eyes lightened to pale blue and a humble smile crept across his face. "You are too kind, Eusebi. I don't know what I'd do without you. You seem to be the only person who will hire me."

"It is how I do the Lord's work. I am the rain and you are the sapling that will become a magnificent tree."

"Yes, but most people view my creations as absurd and crazy." He stared at the golden speckled floor and recalled the shocked faces of the passersby from earlier and the bemused looks of those who attended the Paris World Fair nearly twenty years ago with the same vivid clarity.

Güell lifted his chin with a finger and looked into the pleading eyes of an unsure artist. Gaudí had all the traits that his son lacked: drive, ambition and vision. "That, my boy, is why you're a genius. And in a hundred years, it will be your name that's remembered."

"Do you think so?"

"I know so," he said turning and going to his desk, sitting down and opening a wooden box. "But enough of such talk. How about one of Spain's finest cigars from Cuba?"

Gaudí's worn bones creaked as he gingerly went to the desk and took a seat. "You're supporting Madrid's colonialism buying those, you know?"

Pulling a silver lighter from his vest pocket, Güell puffed a cigar lit and blew out a thick smoke ring. "You've been reading too much Marx. One can be for the people and still enjoy the finer things in life." He turned the opened box towards the architect. "You once indulged."

Gaudí refused with a dismissive wave of the hand. "A sign of an impetuous youth. Besides, it wasn't like rubbing elbows with the Barcelona's finest got me any commissions."

The industrialist found the his friend's candor and honesty refreshing when so many people he knew seemed incapable of an original thought. "I see. We've missed you at mass lately."

"I've been going to the early service. Father Puig has the personality of a cow. Have you ever tried to have a conversation with him? He just looks at you with glassy eyes and moves his mouth."

Güell grinned in agreement at the strange comparison. "Be careful who you tell that to, though. He's a minister's cousin."

"Which minister?"

"Rusiñol."

The architect tiffed in contempt. "Another reason not to go."

"What do you have against Rusiñol?"

"Nothing, other than that fact that he's a spineless politician."

"One who's bringing great prosperity to *Catalunya* if you haven't noticed."

"But not independence."

The industrialist's gray eyes squinted and the many lines of his face hardened. "There will never be independence because *we* don't want it to be." He put out the cigar in a crystal ashtray and stared at the architect. "Really, Antoni, I don't know what's got into you lately with all this separatist talk."

"Is it too much to want my country to be free?"

"You're an idealist and a romantic."

"Am I?"

"Of course, and I envy that. I, on the other hand, am a realist and a pragmatist." Güell stood and looked out onto the courtyard below and watched the driver smoke a cigarette by the black carriage. "And, I tell you this as a proud Catalan - without Spain there is no *Catalunya* and without *Catalunya*, there is no Spain."

"I suppose so. Although, I find it disgusting that I still have to speak *Castellano* to public officials or face jail." Gaudí's skin tingled and warmed. The Holy Spirit possessed him like a sudden gust of wind blowing through a corridor, slamming the door shut to all other thoughts. Sparks flashed and images filled his mind as a piece of the puzzle appeared. Taking a piece of scrap paper and a pencil from Güell's desk, he began to sketch.

The industrialist turned and smiled as he watched his friend work. The passion he possessed was something no amount of money or power could ever buy or achieve.

Güell had tried painting, music and writing and none of them brought out the latent talent he so dearly wished he had. The closest he could ever come to the passion was by being the man who cultivated the artist. He waited for the architect to finish before speaking, "What's that?"

Gaudí showed him a paper with rough lines of arches, pillars, and columns. The angles of their slopes and curves were identical to the inverted chains and sacks of pellets hanging in his studio. "It's an idea I'm working on for the church."

"Ah, I see. It looks almost like a forest." Güell sat down and opened a drawer. "By the way, what do you think of my new toy? A fine piece of German engineering, isn't it?"

"It's better than riding behind a shitting horse." Gaudí set the pencil on the desk and tucked the paper away in the inside pocket of his jacket. "You also have a new employee, I see."

"Who, Jordi?" Güell placed a leather folder on the desk.

"Yes."

"His father was one of my better managers until he had an unfortunate accident at a factory." He paused and sighed like a disappointed teacher who realized their favorite student was just as lazy as the rest. "As you've probably noticed, the boy's not blessed with too much intelligence or looks, so I took him in."

"You're a very generous man."

"No, I am a good catholic and a man of God." He opened the folder. "Speaking of which, how would you like to collaborate with me on a church?"

Gaudí sat up in surprise. "Doesn't Barcelona have enough?"

The architect was one of the few people who made the industrialist laugh. "Not here, at my workers' colony near Sant Boi. We've just finished the school and the hospital. But, as I'm sure you'd agree, what the people need most is a place to worship." He opened the leather folder and pointed to a grainy color photo. "I was thinking here."

Looking at a hillside covered with pine trees, Gaudí's skin tingled and warmed. Pieces of a puzzle controlled by some unseen hand started to form a picture on the blank canvass of his mind. The outline of a building that blended into its natural surroundings came into focus. "I'd love to Eusebi, but I have the Sagrada Familia," he said, feeling the spirit leave as quickly as a summer breeze now that the seed of an idea had been planted.

"I know. You can do both. You're still relatively young."

"Do you have an idea in mind?"

"No, it will be completely your creation." The architect's blue eyes brightened with excitement at the thought of building something from scratch. So far most of commissions he had been offered were to improve on the existing plans of others. After the Sagrada Familia, he would be damned if he'd waste his time using the ideas of lesser men to build something. "Unfortunately, there won't be the same type of budget as with this place," added Güell, dampening the joy. "In fact I'd like you to use the leftover materials from the colony to build it whenever possible."

His patron's frugality surprised Gaudí. "May I ask why?"

"We're entering a new world, Antoni, with more and more competition. I must watch my expenses now." He reached below his desk and took out a bag. "I do have a present for you, though."

The architect's gaunt and wrinkled face revealed a glimpse of the young boy he once was as he pulled out a small mahogany box with brass clasps. He turned it to see two holes on top and the glass lenses of a camera below. "Thank you, Eusebi."

"It's a J. Lancaster I bought the last time I was in London." He lit another cigar. "I thought you could use it to take pictures of all those chains you have dangling."

"It's fantastic. You are truly an angel."

His patron smiled. "No, like you, I am just a vessel for God."

1908

Captured by the Holy Spirit, a bald and white bearded Gaudí worked hunched over a desk to the natural light shining through the windows high on the walls and sketched with such passion that the lines of charcoal bled on the piece of cardboard. Thanks to the recently finished Güell crypt, he was no longer consumed with questions of weight distribution and focused instead on the designs of the three façades and eighteen towers.

The transcendental trance ended like it came - quickly and without warning once the image was down on paper. He stopped drawing and wiped his brow, catching sight of a visitor who stood quietly at the door. He set down his dull stick of charcoal and turned to see Jordi, who was a young man now, but still looked like a gecko.

"Hello, Jordi. How are you?" he said, dusting his hands before taking a cane that hung from the back of his chair.

"I'm fine *Senyor* Gaudí." He rushed over and helped the elderly man steady himself. "And you?"

"Busy."

"Yes, I can see that." Taped to the walls were detailed sketches of the future façades that imagined every centimeter of space engraved with so much religious symbolism, the stones seemed to be melting. "These are very impressive."

Gaudí offered a polite smile and tapped the young boy's arm to show he was ready to leave as he walked towards the smooth steps that led to the inside of the Sagrada Familia's nave.

The surrounding walls were tall enough to cast the entire dust and soot covered floor in a shadow, while the pale daylight slicing through the holes carved for future windows illuminated a forest of white pillars rising into the sky. Walking through the quiet construction site in silence, the men stepped outside into an April day where the sky was a mix of pale blue and gray. The tarps attached to the abandoned scaffolding rustled and flapped in the wind like sails of docked ships as they strolled through mounds of rocks and stacks of slabs of the still unfinished church, now many years behind schedule.

They continued in silence along the paved and tree lined streets until reaching the black carriage, brown rust specks now covering its once sparkling exterior. Looking up at an empty driver's seat, Gaudí asked, "Where's José?"

"*Senyor* Güell had to reduce staff," replied Jordi as he lifted the surprisingly light man into the cabin. "I handle all day-to-day operations now."

***

The preceding eleven years had seen an explosion in automobiles and the smooth asphalt streets of the city teemed with these new machines. Passing buildings free of tarps and scaffolding, the architect noticed that every façade sought to replicate the scenes of nature and medieval *Catalunya* depicted in the poems and essays of Maragall and others. What were once meant to be powerful symbols of a national renaissance had been repeated and diluted becoming the latest bourgeois trend; the power of the images reduced to nothing but a decorative motif for the nouveau riche. He could bare to look no more at the new Barcelona and closed his eyes.

Feeling the cold wind smack his chapped cheeks as they passed Plaça Espanya and left the city, Gaudí pictured the Sagrada Familia in its completed glory - a glowing, everlasting testament to the God Almighty. He prayed for the strength to see it done before his death and for a new infusion of donations. Opening his eyes, he looked back to Barcelona disappearing in the distance and envisioned where the eighteen spindly spires would rise above the skyline. Just imagining it warmed his worn bones.

They drove for nearly an hour before turning off the main road and onto a secondary street that curved up a hill. Three round chimneys towered above a red brick wall and black smoke filled the air to the thunderous sound of machines inside the factories' gray walls. Soon the two and three story buildings of the colony that Gaudi had helped design came into view on the ridge. The car slowed as it entered the village. The first house was made of the same simple red brick as the factory's wall, but its Arabic motif made it fit for a sultan. Sitting on the porch that extended from its second floor was Güell's fat son with a glass of wine, who gave them a wave as they passed by. Gaudí didn't acknowledge him as they drove towards the main street of shops and bars and then on past the workers' apartments, which appeared to be no more than windows and doors carved into a single stone stab.

At the top of a hill, armed soldiers stood guard with rifles and new shiny black automobiles blocked the road, forcing them to stop. Jordi got out and offered the architect a hand down. A crowd of photographers scrambled to ready their bulky cameras for a shot of what was now Barcelona's most famous architect. Gaudí hated the newfound attention. It wasn't like it made people donate to the church. Besides, where were they twenty years ago, he thought, ducking behind Jordi and using him as a human shield from the flashing bulbs.

Free of the press, they strolled up the path side-by-side towards the hazy exterior of the completed crypt behind a row of pine trees. Built from leftover factory bricks, the crypt's gray roof sloped with the hillside, the cement overhang above the entrance forming the mouth of a mysterious cave. Impatient to see the end of this official event, Gaudí didn't take the time to stop and look up at the colorful frescoes adorning the ceiling of the overhang as he quickly shuffled through the slanting pillars and columns to the dark wooden door.

Entering the crypt was like stepping from the darkness of night to the light of day. Smooth granite pillars resembling bones bent and rose, making them appear like skeletal trees. The tall domed brick ceiling was alight in amber from the lamps and the faint sunlight shining through butterfly shaped stained-glass windows. Gaudí stopped to appreciate his design, his spirits lifting like a leaf in a breeze as he pictured the forms and shapes on a much grander scale once the Sagrada Familia was finally completed. The plans and designs were all but done, but as always, there was the question of money.

Only the most respected and powerful people had been invited to the crypt's opening and looking for a familiar face in the crowd, Gaudí saw Güell standing by a massive oyster shell that served as the aspersoria. Next to him was a short man whose elegance made the industrialist look like a pauper. "Antoni! I didn't think you'd make it," his patron said. "May I present you to the King of Spain?"

"I am a big fan of yours." The short man spoke in the official language of the Spanish nation, *Castellano*.

Kneeling in respect, Gaudí replied in Catalan, "How do you do your majesty?"

The king's eyes twitched at the linguistic insult. "Did you not just hear who I am?"

"Yes, your honor. And I speak to you as a Catalan loyal to the King of Spain."

The few white strands of hair atop Güell's head stood erect in shock as he shoved Gaudí to the side. While the king was generally tolerant of linguistic freedom, his Spanish pride made not addressing him in the official language another matter entirely. "Sorry, your majesty, he's under a lot of stress," the blushing industrialist said as he pushed the architect towards the door and the gray day.

Clear of the mosaic overhang and the armed guards, the two men stood by the side of the crypt's brick tower where a single wall stood without the support of flying buttresses. A furious Güell did everything in his power not to yell, "What's wrong with you, Antoni?"

"What?" Gaudí feigned innocence. "I was just being pragmatic and realistic, like you. Is the king so thinned skinned I must speak in Spanish even when he visits *Catalunya*?"

The industrialist's face reddened, bordering on purple. "Are you crazy? This is not some silly prank. People have been executed for less!"

"The king won't execute me. I'm too famous."

"You just don't understand, Antoni. Now is not a good time to be stirring the pot."

"What is it, Eusebi?"

His patron's face was no longer red but pale and lined with worry. "I'm afraid we have to halt construction on this church."

"For how long?"

"Until I can sort things out. I'm trying to gain access to the Morocco territories." Güell stopped and looked coldly at the architect. "I was also going to ask the king to put a word in with the Vatican to see if they couldn't help with the Sagrada Familia."

"Forgive me, Eusebi. I wasn't aware."

"How could you be? You are just an artist!" Güell repeatedly tapped his skull. "You don't live in reality. You live in your head."

"And what is the reality?"

"The reality is, while we Catalans may have a different language and culture, in the end we are all Spanish and we must respect our king, as it has been for centuries."

Gaudí looked at his benefactor. Underneath his elegant veneer of national pride, religious piety and artistic sophistication, he was no different than the others who only thought about lining their pockets at the expense of the people and their principles. "You're such a hypocrite."

"Am I? Why? Because I understand that history cannot be changed and that without Spain's protection we would have been invaded by France? Just look at *Perpinyà* and North *Catalunya* to see how that has worked out." Güell's face softened. He truly did love Gaudí more than his son and understood men of art and beauty couldn't begin to comprehend the dirty and ugly world of politics and business. "Honestly Antoni, I wish it were different, just like I'm sure you wish you didn't need people like me, but it is what it is."

As Gaudí looked into Güell's pale and moist eyes, his body warmed as if he were sitting by a fire on a cold winter's day at his parents' *masia* near Reus. And just like when he looked into the flickering flames and saw images of spring days as a healthy young boy sprinting up a gravel path to his mother, so did he see pictures now, although they were still photos shot by a camera. The first was of Güell coming into his old studio beaming a confident smile before it quickly flipped to another picture of him introducing himself to Gaudí. Then another image appeared and then another, creating a moving picture of times spent doing nothing but talking after which Gaudi always came back inspired to serve his second most important client. And with one last pop and flash, the images stopped and he realized - it wasn't the industrialist's money that made him a famous architect, but his friendship. "I'm truly sorry, Eusebi."

A forgiving smile crossed his patron's face and he laid a hand on Gaudí's shoulder. "It's alright. What's done is done. Now no more talk. Go home and I'll see if I can't smooth some easily ruffled Spanish feathers. How's that sound?"

Gaudí stepped away and stared at his old friend. There was a question he had wanted to ask him since that day twenty years ago at his old studio. "Eusebi?"

"Yes."

"I know we are both men of God, but why me? Are there not others?"

"Because in a hundred years you'll be the reason my name will be remembered."

"Do you honestly think so?"

"Trust me. You will be known as Barcelona's greatest artist and the whole city will owe a debt to the extraordinary talents of Antoni Gaudí and his erstwhile benefactor, Eusebi Güell."

The architect smiled.

"Now, come on. I've got a new idea I want to discuss with you," the industrialist said as he led Gaudí away from the crypt of simple gray bricks and pitched an idea to turn some land he owned at the base of the Barcelona foothills into the grandest residential neighborhood ever built. He said it had the potential to make all their money problems disappear and called the project: Parc Güell.

Barcelona Gothic

"**H**ello, you sent me an email about a room for rent," Alex said excited at the possibility of escaping his current windowless dwelling.

"Yes, I saw your ad on *Loquo*," replied a deep monotone voice. "You must come today if interested. It's number four Urquinaona, 2-1. Do you know where that is?"

"I think so."

"Good. Come in an hour." Click.

New to Barcelona from Asturias, Alex had only known Urquinaona as the stop to change from the red to the yellow line on the way to the beach. As the station's escalator brought him to the surface, his face lit up at the sight of one of the few shaded squares in the city that was also a stone's throw from Plaça Catalunya. Great location, he thought, crossing the street and passing the yellow metal barrier of some roadwork where two men stood smoking watching a third in a hole.

Near the end of the square, sandwiched between a bank and an Irish bar, was a large wooden door. Alex's eyes immediately set on the two brass knockers molded into the shape of smooth and slender hands that hung limp and held what appeared to be an apple in their finger tips. Such ornamental fixtures were not that uncommon in Barcelona and above the dark wooden door was another common sight – a piece of chiseled stone. In this case, rather than the more popular rose or angel, it was a roaring lion's head.

The gray stones of the building were embedded with glittering green specks and its design was typical of the modernist architecture found throughout the L'Eixample district of the city. Many of the artistic façades sought inspiration in nature with stone columns made to look like trees and patio doors that opened onto balconies with floral iron railings. This one hearkened back to the Middle Ages, designed to resemble a castle. On either side of a rectangular balcony, protruding like glass and steel turrets, were the rounded outside windows of the first two stories. Their stone roofs served as patios for the third floor with their straight iron railings and glass doors, while above was a row of arched windows and a shared, narrow balcony that looked onto the plaça. The thought of living in such a place made Alex hope he was the first, and the last, to visit as he pressed the button on the intercom.

A crackle and a muffled "Si?" came through the speaker a second later.

"It's Alex." A crackle and a long buzz sounded as he entered a small, light gray entrance built more for a palace than an apartment building. Ivory colored frescoes ran down the middle of the sidewalls and ended at a polished rosewood and glass divider. Through the open door in the middle was a lobby adorned in more wood in an auburn light from a hanging chandelier. At the back sat a single red elevator between the first flight of stone steps and an empty booth.

The wooden elevator was about the size of a coffin and Alex closed his eyes to fight off feelings of claustrophobia. Imagining the rolling green countryside of northern Spain, he lost himself in the lush scenery as the rickety box slowly chugged up to the cranks of a struggling chain. An abrupt stop a minute later signaled a safe arrival. He pulled the doors in to open, twisted out and yanked them shut.

"Hello, I am Sergi."

It was the same deep monotone voice from earlier and Alex turned to find it belonged to a thin, hunched man in his mid-thirties whose skin was so pale, it looked gray. "Hey, I'm Alex."

"Nice to meet you. Please come in."

"Nice to meet you, too. This is a fantastic building." Inside the entryway for the flat and the one opposite from it was a stain-glass rendition of the patron saint of *Catalunya*. Alex was on the verge of commenting on it, when a bronze plaque for a doctor on the opposite door caught his eye. "That's handy in case I get really sick."

"The doctor died a few years ago and his son is trying to sell the office and our flat."

"Really?" Alex didn't like the thought of looking for another place anytime soon. He had done it twice already in his year in Barcelona and he hated the looking, running around, interviewing and waiting. It was worse than looking for a job.

"Don't worry. No one wants it with the economic crisis and the housing market the way it is." Sergi opened the front door and they entered a small foyer after which was a long corridor that stretched back and ended at thick, purple curtains covering French doors. "My last flat mate liked to go on the balcony and throw firecrackers at people, so now no one can go out there."

"Um, okay," replied Alex thinking the story a little strange.

"This is the kitchen." The first door on the left revealed a room bigger than many actual *flats* Alex had seen. The tan and brown color scheme reminded him of something from the nineteen-fifties and the grease splattered walls and appliances showed it was in need of a good cleaning. Still, it came with a stove, refrigerator, microwave and an oven all in the same location.

"This is great," was his response.

"Good." Sergi moved the tour along to a large closet that stored a washer, a dryer and various opened boxes of detergent. Next was a freshly cleaned bathroom that was big enough to fit a tub, two sinks, a toilet and a bidet. Finally, at the end of the long corridor on either side of the thick curtains were two doors. "This is my office," Sergi said pointing at a closed smoked glass door to the left. "And, this is the room."

It was bright and spacious with a large oak desk, a queen-size bed and enough closet space for a drag queen. But what really got Alex's attention was the area inside of the building's glass and iron turrets where a plush chair looked out the ceiling high bay-windows onto the shaded plaça below. "It's perfect," he said.

"You want it?"

"At the price in the email?"

"Yes and no deposit. But you must stay one month. You cannot leave before. Is that clear? It is not always easy to find quiet people."

"No problem. I think I'll be staying a while."

His answer caused Sergi's thin lips to curl into a satisfied grin. "Good. Here are the keys."

"Okay, flat mate. How many people live in the building?"

"We are the only ones. The rest are offices or vacant."

"I see. So, how long have you lived here?"

"Fifteen years. I was the doctor's last flat mate. His wife had just died and he wanted company. That's why the rent is so cheap."

"And what do you do, if you don't mind me asking?"

"I am a programmer."

"Oh, me too! But I'm looking to get more into design and animation."

"Yes, I know. You mentioned that in your ad. Maybe one day I'll show you what I am working on, but right now I must leave town for a while. You can move in whenever you want."

"Okay, and thanks."

"No problem. Just remember, it is an old flat so it sometimes makes strange noises."

***

The arrival of dusk dulled the embedded green specks leaving the building a singular raven black and the lack of lights in the windows made it stand out amid the brightness of the bustling plaça. Setting down his two stuffed, bulging suitcases, Alex rolled his sore shoulders and fiddled in his pockets for the keys. The steady stream of pedestrians and the music from the Irish bar next door reminded him why he'd wanted to live in the city-center.

The solid lock clanked open. He pushed the thick wooden door and stepped into the entrance. The only light came from the red elevator at the far back and Alex struggled with the bags as he rolled them past the frescoes, up the three stairs and through the rosewood divider to the empty lobby. Not trusting the rickety elevator to handle the excess weight, he braved the stairs and slowly trudged up the stone steps, anxious and excited to spend his first night in his great, new flat.

His arms burned and shook by the time he reached the room. Letting out a deep breath, he set the heavy suitcases down and strolled to the area by the rounded bay window. The chair looked so comfy. He sat down and leaned his head back to relax, gazing upon a sky that was a deep purple with the end of dusk and the beginning of night. The street lamps in the plaça below had all faded on, shading the black trees and benches in a soft white light. The bright and bustling Via Laietana came alive in the yellow and red lights of traffic and in the not too far off distance were the illuminated stone-spires of the Gothic Cathedral. Beyond them were five blinking lights of planes lining up to land over the dark castle on Montjuïc Mountain. Alex thought, what a view, as he closed his eyes and fell asleep to the quiet hum of the street.

***

It all began as a faint murmur in the distant background of a dream. He was the doctor and his blond, American friend, Dorothy, the patient. As she lay unconscious in a chair by the window, he stood over and looked at her longingly. He had never had such a beautiful girl in his room. Imagining the possibilities, a sinister smile crossed his face and he snapped off a latex glove. The murmur rose to a faint rumble. He stroked her smooth cheek. It was so soft, he could just bite it. Low growls and scratches stopped him from acting on his desires. Looking around, he saw nothing so he went to kiss her closed mouth.

***

The raging bark of a vicious dog erupted, opening his eyes. "*Coño!*" he cursed sitting up in bed, shaking from the dream. "Sergi, did you forget to tell me about the dog?"

No reply.

"Serrrrggggiiiii!"

The growls and snarls faded from the hall outside his room. Alex counted to ten. There was no sign of the snarling beast. Taking a deep breath, he grabbed the heavy English-Spanish dictionary from his desk and crept across the room, slowly opening the door. The smoked glass of his flat mate's office across the hall glowed a pale white and Alex knocked. "Sergi, are you here?"

He heard no reply, so he went for the handle, only to find it gone. Bending down and looking through the hole, he saw the light belonged to a ceiling projector and heard the humming of computer fans. "Must just be some program of his," Alex said aloud in an effort to reassure himself and returned to his room, setting the dictionary back on the desk. The old pipes groaned and the building moaned, but he heard no more growls or scratches as he lay awake and waited for morning.

***

The Irish bar next door was the size of a small church and decorated appropriately with organ pipes and stain-glass windows adorning its brick walls. Calling Dorothy during his lunch break, Alex asked if she wanted to meet there for happy-hour. She instantly agreed citing a stressful week teaching Spanish and Catalan kids. They had met through a language exchange some months earlier and he had fallen in love with her tall, blond, American good looks at first sight. Since then, he had become her drinking buddy and sounding board when it came to all issues pertaining to men. Seeing her on a wooden stool, the image of Dorothy at his mercy flashed and his stomach sunk. "You okay, Alex?" she asked.

"Yes, sorry. I didn't sleep well last night." He told her about the dog, but left out the dream.

"There's always something with you. What you wanna drink?"

"I think I'll have a beer and a *chupito*. I want to get drunk tonight."

A few tequila shots and multiple beers later, he had accomplished his mission. "Wha' time is it?" Alex slurred.

"It's still early, almost two. Why?"

"I should go home and sleep."

"What about the dog?"

"Fuck the dog! I'll kick it out the window onto the *plaça*."

"Alex!"

"I'm too drunk to care, Dorothy. We see each other soon?"

"Sure, call me if anything strange happens."

"I'm sure nothing will." Staggering out the bar and walking next door to his flat, he threw up three times under the gaze of the stone lion before lifting his head and spitting. Feeling better but still too wasted to think, he let instincts take over and guide him though the door and the lobby, up the stairs and into his flat, down the long hall and into his room where he passed out to silence.

***

Over the next few weeks, Alex and Dorothy met every night at the Irish bar. He had gotten used to the old flat's creaks and moans and forgotten all about strange dog until the loud bang of a hammer and stomping footsteps rudely woke him up one Saturday morning. Walking out of his room hung-over, he discovered Sergi with a towel wrapped around waist. The few black strands of hair on his head were slicked back, making him look like a bald, soaked rat. "What's up? You're home I hear," Alex said.

"Yes. Sorry to wake you. I was having problems with the door to my office. I lost the knob."

"I see." Alex was too tired to comment on such a bizarre explanation. "Sergi, are there animals in this building?"

"Animals?"

"Yes, I heard something my first night."

163

"Not in this building; maybe in the hostel next door. Like I said, it's an old apartment, so the noise carries."

"I see."

"Look, I must get dressed. Is everything okay?"

Mulling over what to say, Alex replied, "Yeah, things are good. I'm all settled in."

***

The following Thursday he returned home burned out from a hard day's work. Fixing himself a can of soup and a drink, he sat at the small kitchen table and stared at the placement of the flowered tiles on the walls. Consisting of five mustard petals around a brown center, they were sometimes clustered in a square, in a circle, or in a diagonal line. Sometimes, they simply stood alone. The number of grease-splattered plain ones that separated them ranged from one to ten. And no matter how he looked at it, he saw no logical pattern for why they were where they were.

How long he had zoned out attempting to figure out the riddle of the tiles, Alex did not know. He could barely keep his eyes open. His cold soup sat untouched on the table so he got up and dumped it in the sink, set the bowl atop the stack of dirty dishes, and walked out into a long corridor. He got no more than five steps before the bulb midway down flashed, popped and went dark.

The lights of the city and the moon shone through the large bay window of his room casting a flickering light on the walls and floor. The hall seemed to be stretching, pushing the room further away as the lights dimmed. Surrounded by darkness, the walk had become a long march and his legs labored with each step like when he had to change from the yellow to green line at Passeig de Gracia with its three block tunnel. Finally making it to his door, he fell to his hands and knees and crawled into his room.

Struggling to his feet, Alex looked to the window and shivered. A slender man in a white smock stood at the side of a doctor's chair. His back to Alex, he blocked all but the legs of the person with him. Judging by the slender and smooth calves, Alex believed it to be a woman. "Hey," he said.

The man didn't answer nor move.

"Who are you?"

No response.

Alex didn't know what to do, run or try to see who the man was. He chose to do neither and stayed put. "What do you want?" he shouted.

The man slowly turned around. His loose skin hung from his skull like drapes and he had a black mustache so thin and straight it looked drawn. Stepping aside, he revealed a woman whose beauty made her sleeping body glow like the wooden and golden statues of the Virgin Mary at the Santa Maria del Mar. "Isn't she lovely? Haven't you dreamed of having a woman like this at your finger tips, Alex?"

***

A bloodcurdling scream and a series of vicious barks caused Alex to fall out of the chair and onto the sticky kitchen floor. He listened for the woman or the dog. He heard only the steady drip of the leaking faucet plop against the stack of dirty plates. His eyes focused the flowered tiles, where there once was a circle, there was only one and where there once a square, there was none. He shifted focus to the counter and his jaw dropped at the sight of a carving knife hacked into an apple. Jumping up, he sprinted out the door to a flat-shaking slam.

He immediately went to the Irish bar for a drink. "You look like you've seen a ghost," said Dorothy with a gulp of beer. She had become a regular barfly there since the arrival of the new Argentinean bartender.

"I think I have – Well, not seen, but...but heard," Alex replied taking a shot of tequila.

"Really! I love ghosts. I did the haunted tours in London and Prague."

"Well, I don't and I need another shot."

"What happened?"

"I told you about the dog, right?" Alex detailed the night's events while smoking almost all of Dorothy's cigarettes.

"And you're sure your flat mate's not home?"

"I haven't seen him. Besides, I was in the kitchen the whole time."

"Hmm, that is strange. But I'm sure there's a logical explanation." Dorothy sipped on her beer and her eyes sparkled at a thought. "I'll stay the night with you."

"What?"

"It'll be fun."

"Are you crazy?"

"Come on, Alex." She punched him in the arm for encouragement.

"I don't know..."

"You have to go back and get your stuff anyway. Plus, I just got pepper spray."

"What?"

"Yeah, I didn't tell you? I got my purse snatched in *El Raval* last week. I'm not getting robbed again, you know?"

"Barcelona is going to shit."

"Don't be so negative! Can I stay or what?"

Alex wanted to refuse and find a cheap hotel to stay in, but the enthusiastic look in Dorothy's eyes told him that wasn't an option. He was never able to say no to her, which explained the increased frequency of hangovers he had been waking up with in the mornings.

***

At the door to his flat a sense of dread not unlike the times he'd had to tell his father about a poor mark at school, flooded through him. Looking at the image of St. George standing above the vanquished dragon, he called on the courage to say what he had been feeling since they left the pub. "I really don't think we should, Dorothy."

"Come on." She put her soft hand on his and inserted the key into the lock. "Ghosts can't hurt you, I promise."

"How do you know?"

"I told you, I'm like a total ghost-freak. I think I've seen every documentary on the Internet." She slowly forced him to turn the key. The lock clicked and the hinges squeaked. They stepped into a silent flat and the lights from Alex's room flickered on the walls and the floor. A draft whooshed down the corridor, slamming all open doors, bringing pitch blackness. They shrieked and jumped into each other's arms. "That was freaky, huh?" Dorothy laughed nervously as they entered the kitchen.

With the flip of a switch, a bright light shone that forced their eyes to adjust. When they did, there was neither an apple nor a knife to be found. Meanwhile, the flowered tiles were back to their original random places. Rubbing his eyes, Alex said, "I swear there really was a knife," as doubt in his own sanity set in.

"I believe you. No one could've made that up," she replied following him down the corridor.

"Aren't you the least bit scared?"

"Of course, but it's like totally exciting too, right?"

"Not really," he said now standing at his closed door. His heart pounded and his palms became clammy at the thought of what awaited on the other side.

"Shall we?" Dorothy didn't wait for an answer, turned the knob and entered the room. "All clear," she said and Alex quickly followed her inside.

He immediately went to the switch for the floor lamp, a spark and a pop and the bulb went dead. "*Coño,*" he cursed.

"It's alright. We can see fine. Do you have something I can wear?"

Walking to the large closet, he took out clean sweats and a t-shirt. "Here you go."

"Thanks. Going to the bathroom to change."

"Okay." Alone in his room, Alex went to the chair by the window. Barcelona was enveloped in a light drizzle that blurred the white lights of the plaça and distorted the illuminated spires of the Gothic Cathedral. Looking at the silhouette of the castle atop Montjuïc Mountain, he saw the doctor's face flash in the glass. A gust of wind smacked the window and rattled the steel frames. He stumbled back and slammed into the edge of the desk.

"Are you okay?" asked Dorothy looking at a face whiter than the moon.

"Not really," He clenched his stinging thigh. "Look, Dorothy..."

"Alex, don't say anything. Let's just go to bed and see what happens. At least we have each other if anything gets too crazy."

"But aren't you worried I might try something?"

"You? You're too nice. Besides, I'm a light sleeper."

***

Waking from a deep sleep, Alex got up and slowly strode to the other side of the bed, moving with a calmness that suggested he had done it before. He stood over Dorothy and watched her sleep, blissfully unaware and spread out like a star. The calmness gave way to the giddy excitement of doing something bad for the first time and his skin tingled.

He snapped off a latex glove, unveiling a slender hand made of brass. Holding it to the window, slowly moving the fingers, he admired its shiny beauty and smooth perfection. The whiskers above his lip thickened into the beginnings of a mustache and he smiled sinisterly. The giddiness grew to a buzzing rush at the thought of doing something dirty and his blood raced through his veins. Gently stroking her smooth cheek with the back of his cold hand, he listened to her murmur. He imagined sick and demented acts. The rush reached a burning desire to act on his dark fantasies and his eyes widened in anticipation. He could wait no more. Bending down, he kissed her slightly open mouth.

A growl vibrated off the walls. He stood and turned. A snarling Yorkshire terrier crouched at the foot of bed. Alex went to kick it out the window. The dog's claws scratched the floor as it skidded and charged.

***

The pain pulsating in Alex's leg woke him up with his mouth open to scream. He felt a few drops of warm blood trickling from where he had run into the table. Out of the corner of his eye, he saw Dorothy safely curled up in the fetal position. So much for being a light sleeper, he thought before his mind returned to his leg and the dream - was it the flat or him? After all, he hadn't been with a girl in over a year and this might be the manifestation of pent-up sexual frustration. It couldn't be that. He was used to going long periods without sex. It had to be the flat and the key was Sergi.

After ransacking the kitchen drawers for some tools, he went to smoked glass door of Sergi's office. Staring at a hole where a handle was supposed to be, he kicked it to test the lock - it didn't budge. He gritted his teeth and jabbed a long flathead screwdriver between the door and the frame, pushed and pried. The wood splintered. He took the hammer and banged the screwdriver's handle like a construction worker on a caffeine rush. Splinters turned to cracks. Lowering his shoulder, he slammed into the door and crashed through, the shot of pain he felt reminding him that this wasn't a dream. "What's going on, Alex?" yawned Dorothy.

"I'm getting to the bottom of this," he declared entering an office that smelled of stale vomit and old booze. The projector overhead beamed a streaming code on a black screen consisting of strange red letters and symbols. It was unlike any computer script or language Alex had ever studied or seen.

"Looks like someone else was here." Dorothy pointed to a desk best described as a disaster and two empty glasses next to a half-drunk bottle of whiskey.

"Maybe he has a friend?"

"Hmm, maybe." She took a book from the shelf and read the back and cover. "My Catalan's not all that great, but I think this is about magic and spells."

"This is insane." Alex stormed out with his mind racing at what it all meant. Back in his room, he took an empty suitcase from the closet. "Dorothy, we really should find someplace else to stay the rest of the night."

"Alex – It's almost five in the morning. There's no point in leaving now. Why don't we Google this place and see what we can find out?"

"I just want to leave, you know?"

"You're not the tiniest bit curious?"

"No," Alex threw a pile of clothes still on the hangers onto the bed.

"Can I search?"

"Go ahead. I'm getting out of here."

"Let's see." Dorothy typed in the address and hit enter - nothing but listings for apartment and hotel rentals. "Hmm … What else do we know?"

"There was a doctor who lived here. Maybe he has something to do with it."

"What makes you say that?"

"Some strange dreams I've been having." Alex zipped up the first suitcase and went for a second.

"You know his name"

"No."

The door slammed. Alex dropped the clothes in his arms as every hair on his body hair prickled. Slowly turning around, he found Sergi standing in the shadows of the entrance with a carving knife. "What do you think you're doing, Alex?"

"I'm leaving."

"No you aren't. You must stay one month." Sergi stepped into the light. "You shouldn't have broken into my office."

"What the fuck, man? Have you been here all this time? Did you stick that knife through an apple?"

"Do not accuse me of such things," he said stabbing the long blade in the air at Alex for emphasis.

"If you didn't – Who did? "

Jeremy Holland

"My special friend. I think you've already met, but let me properly introduce you. Your room used to be his private office."

Alex stared at Sergi extend his hand as if someone other than the wall was next to him. "What the fuck are you talking about? There's no one there."

"He's being shy, but you *have* seen him, haven't you?"

"Are you crazy?" Dorothy shouted as she inched towards the desk.

Sergi flashed the knife and hissed, "You! Don't move."

"You can't stop us from leaving." Alex showed the screwdriver.

Sergi held up the bigger blade. "Yes, I can, and I will."

"I don't understand."

"You see, as long as I bring him someone once a month to – let's say – play with, I can stay here." He explained how the ghost preferred women tenants, but settled on Alex after Sergi had failed to land any in three months. He nodded to Dorothy. "But he's glad he did now with her here."

"And the dog?" Alex asked.

Sergi's face softened. "It belonged to his last patient. It started barking and woke up the owner. It was the only time he ever killed anything."

"You made a deal with a ghost to stay here?"

A wide smile crossed Sergi's pale face revealing a mouth full of yellow teeth. "Yes, how else can a person afford to live in Barcelona?"

The sentence hung in the air like a bad punch line and Alex gazed into his flat mate's black eyes.

"You're insane."

"Am I? Or is it you who's crazy?"

The two of them locked in a high-noon stare. Dorothy seized the moment and grabbed the thick concise Spanish-English dictionary on the desk, flinging it like a discus at Sergi as he made a menacing first move towards Alex. The loud smack of heavy book hitting the tiled floor made him jump back and he scanned the room. His eyes fixed on the blue book at his feet.

Alex gripped the screwdriver and made his move. Sergi slashed the knife at him and hissed like a rabid cat. "Easy there," Alex said stepping back with his hands up.

Sergi's eyes wide with rage, he turned to Dorothy. "You've asked for it now, bitch."

A steady stream of pepper spray hissed but he didn't scream. Dorothy jumped on Alex's bed and pressed the nozzle, pushing towards the crazy Spaniard until he dropped the knife, clutched his face and collapsed onto the ground. She stopped spraying. "Come on," she said, taking Alex's hand and dragging him to the long corridor away from the eye-stinging fumes of the pepper spray and the wailing ex-flat mate. "You can stay at my place. Don't worry; I won't pull a knife on you, unless you don't do the dishes."

The words were followed by one last slam of a door as they ran out of the flat, down the stairs, and through the dark lobby to the street. Dawn had set on Barcelona, covering the plaça across the street in a fine mist and at a traffic signal, a taxi with a green light signaling its availability waited. They jumped in the back. "*Rambla Poblenou*," Dorothy said.

"*Vale*," replied the driver as Alex turned and watched the dark, castle-like building of Plaça Urquinaona recede from sight. Finally far enough away from the terrifying place to feel safe, he turned and looked at the driver's reflection in the rear-view mirror. Above his lip was a black mustache so thin and straight it looked drawn.

The Sound of Barcelona

It's the drilling that wakes you up at nine o'clock on a Saturday morning. The same sputtering, spinning and wheezing that's been your weekend alarm for the last six years. Where it comes from, who knows? Some days it's the apartment next door, others the one above or below. What on earth are they doing? It doesn't matter. You just want it to stop and pound on the wall, cursing at the top of your lungs. It's the weekend for fuck's sake! The drilling ceases at the bang of a bored hole. Five seconds of silence for a snooze before the hammering commences. It's time to get up whether you want to or not.

You're tired. The garbage trucks collecting the trash, the tricked-out scooters roaring down the street, the shouts and screams of drunks stumbling home make a decent night's sleep impossible. The morning drilling and hammering make weekend lie-ins rarer than a sunny day in April and a full time job means there's no sleeping in during the week. Staggering out of bed in a groggy and grumpy mood, you start the count down until nap-time like a metro clock: *Proper siesta* minus six hours, fifty-nine minutes, thirteen seconds and counting.

At the elevator outside the flat, the light by the call buttons glows orange, indicating an open door somewhere in the building. Two minutes pass and still no sign of it. The drill has started again and is accompanied by Freddy Mercury wailing from a stereo at full volume. The stairs seem like the best option. Two flights down, the outside white iron-mesh gate of the elevator is flung open. The two red interior wooden doors are pushed in. There's no one around so you enter a cab the size of clothes chest and pull the squeaky gate closed. A door to a flat flies open and woman runs out. "What are you doing?" she cries in Spanish, flinging open the gate to stop the elevator from leaving.

You have no problems responding in the language and reply, "I'm going down."

"You can't."

"Why?"

"I'm almost ready to leave" she says. "Just five more minutes. Let me explain, I have to..."

The drill for an alarm clock leaves little patience for an explanation and you reply, "*Bueno,* by the time you finish getting ready, the elevator will have gone down and come up again," slamming the white gate and the two wooden doors before pushing the protruding button for the lobby.

The rickety elevator comes to an abrupt stop and the doors fly open. A heavy-set man bathed in a cheap cologne storms in. The urge to give him a shove rises, but you think better of it, take a deep breath, and squeeze between him and the elevator wall, stepping into a white lobby and a pleasant surprise. There's none of the jack-hammering, banging or shouting that usually vibrates off the stone walls at this time of day. You go outside and the pavement is free of metal plates, yellow barriers and construction workers. There's no obvious difference between two years ago and now but it's not the moment to contemplate the reason for the racket or why it took so long. Instead, it's the time to renounce atheism and thank God that the noise has finally finished bringing with it peace and quiet. People sit on shaded benches under trees at the square across the street and in the powder blue sky, a flock of escaped parakeets fly. A cup of coffee seems like the perfect way to start this beautiful day.

Three seconds later, a pile of dog shit on the ground provokes frustration at the Spanish unwillingness to pick up after their animals. It's a short lived rise. Suddenly, your people-sense tingles and warns of an incoming pedestrian bent on a collision. It's an impeccably dressed elderly Spanish woman with dyed blue hair pushing a shopping cart. Her unblinking eyes are the size of coasters behind thick glasses and she sucks on the bottom lip of a toothless mouth in determination. She heads straight for you like a slow moving, heat-seeking missile. You veer left to avoid impact. She's locked on target, steers her shopping cart and mirrors the movement. Hugging the stone wall of a building, brushing against a brass hand for a knocker, you give her the entire pavement to pass. She still insists on a collision. It has essentially become a game of pedestrian chicken, with people replacing cars and a random choice of targets. Her aim is to win. She's eighty and you're not even half that, so you give way.

There's no time to think about why the Spanish are incapable of walking in a straight line. The man ahead has decided to stop and light a smoke, leaving you less than a second to avoid slamming into his back. Dropping a spin move like a football player shedding his marker on a corner kick, you join the pedestrian flow and settle behind a couple leisurely walking hand-in-hand anxious to find a quiet place to drink a coffee. They loudly discuss the state of Spanish politics and an opening appears to their left. They move in unison to stop you from passing, as if their matching square-rimmed glasses contain rear-view mirrors. Some space between them and a woman smoking and pushing a baby stroller appears to their right. Again, they deny you from overtaking them as their topic changes to lunch later that day with some friends. Sometimes walking in Barcelona is more frustrating than driving in L.A.

A red light presents an opportunity for some separation. Across the street is the famous Casa Batlló by Gaudi. An homage to Saint George, the curved purple roof is the back and head of a dragon, the gray cross-shaped chimney is the hilt of the plunged sword and the bone-shaped window frames are the skeletons of those devoured by the beast. The traffic light changes from red to green. Your focus shifts from the building to a bus barreling through the red the light. The next car stops and you jump out of the block and sprint ahead before the rest of the people even realize it's safe to cross.

Still in need of a coffee, you duck into a bright Spanish bar, take a stool at the counter and nod at the bartender. The man working finishes giving a single glass a thorough cleaning and places it on a rack. He then walks over and counts a full box of potato chips after which he carefully inspects the cash register tape.

You say, "Excuse me."

He straightens each of the *tapas* plates under the glass covering before finally sauntering over. "What?"

"*Un cortado.*"

He leaves and you wait.

A deep, long hack and a cackling cough announces the arrival of an old Spanish man. His thinning gray hair slicked back, he smokes a pungent Ducado cigarette and wears a silver, three-day-old beard on a brown, weathered face. The bar is empty but he sits next to you and blows out a thick cloud of smoke. The bartender delivers your espresso topped with milk in a large shot glass. "*Hombre*, give me a *carajillo*," the man demands in a husky voice.

The bartender offers no reply, readies the espresso machine and grabs a bottle of brandy for the order. "Politicians are sons of whores," the old man says in Spanish.

You agree, but avoid religious and political discussions and silently stir the sugar into the coffee.

He looks at you. The silence leaves him confused. He tries another approach to initiate a conversation. "Where *jou* from?" he asks in accented English.

"America." You drink the shot of coffee.

"America! I know America. I was there many years ago."

"Did you like it?"

"No. The cities are ugly and the food was terrible. Why you eat only hamburgers?"

"We eat other things."

"When I was there – only hamburgers. You smoke?" He offers a cigarette.

"No, thanks." You wave at the bartender and ask for the check, "*La cuenta, por favor.*"

He presses to have a chat and steps in so his head is under your chin. His breath smells like watered down whiskey left in a glass later used as an ashtray. "You like Spain? Spain is the best, no?"

"Yes, I do." You count the exact change necessary and step back from the man.

He presses forward. "You like Spanish food? It's the best, no?"

"Yeah, take care."

You run outside and gulp the fresh air. The buzz from the strong coffee has you ready to do something and makes a nap a remote possibility. On the to-do list for the last month has been to buy that all-on-one printer/scanner/fax advertised in all the newspapers. A wall of smoking teenagers blocks the metro entrance while at the red bus stop, a group of elderly Spanish ladies wait and chat. Strangers, they talk more as if they are neighbors. And, like the one who challenged you to a game of chicken, they are all immaculately dressed in freshly ironed blouses and skirts. The late morning sun leaves most people perspiring, but their perfectly made-up faces are completely free of one bead of sweat. At the arrival of the long red TMB bus, they let out a joyous cry and anxiously jostle for position, throwing the occasional elbow and hip-check to be the first in line.

The doors bend in to open. In no rush, you stand at the back of the tangled mob and wait for order to gradually form out of the chaos. Boarding is a slow process. People slowly funnel in, fiddle in their bags and pockets for their tickets to punch or the change to pay the driver and then proceed the minimal distance possible to secure a space. By the time the ticket machine beeps with your ticket, the front of the aisle is full and the bus is at the next stop. On the plus side, there are plenty of free seats at the back.

The bus is soon standing room only and full of grating chatter. A teenage girl two seats away talks on her cell about her boyfriend loud enough for the driver to understand. Behind her is a serious looking young man who offers his detailed analysis of the new Woody Allen movie to his girlfriend. She shows little interest, checks her reflection in the window and tosses her hair. Not being fluent in Spanish makes it easy for you to tune out the inane conversations taking place and the mind jumps to the future, imagining a dark room and a bed. *Proper siesta* minus three-hours, twenty-minutes, forty-four seconds and counting.

***

At a two-story electronics store near Ronda Sant Antoni, there are no signs. Monitors sit next to washers and dryers; televisions are placed with coffee machines. Searching for someone to help find the printer section, you see employees appear and disappear in a flash and give chase like a cat after a fly, until finally cornering a skinny teenage boy with a mullet.

You say, "I'm looking for..."

"We don't have it," he replies.

"I haven't told you what yet."

"We still don't have it."

"It's that all-in-one printer advertised everywhere."

"I told you, we don't have it. It doesn't even exist."

"How does it not exist? It's advertised in every newspaper."

"Look, it doesn't exist, okay?"

"Do you have anything similar?"

"No. Check another store." He struts away as if he's just made a million dollar sale, ending any desire to deal with Spanish service for the day. The time is now one o'clock. The stomach rumbles with hunger. Most restaurants don't open for another half-an-hour at least. To kill time, you head to the L'Eixample district to check out the buildings on the way to the little bodega near Provença.

The red-bus leaving the stop means a twenty minute minimum wait for the next one, so you decide to take the metro. A flood of people hurry up the stairs and a man with a sour face looks like he wishes to play pedestrian chicken. Unlike the woman from this morning, he isn't elderly. There's no giving way and you grab the banister and puff out your chest to remind him who has leverage. He gives in with a grunt and goes around.

It's a short-lived victory. Rushing passengers stampede from both the entrance and the exit doors. You pause, think, and pick out the best lane to take. Weaving through the people like midfielder from Barcelona Football Club, you juke the oncoming waves of commuters and spin around anyone who stops suddenly. The aim is to make it to the row of three turnstiles without touching anyone. You succeed and find a man repeatedly trying to make his stripped ticket work at the first turnstile. Three people line up to pass through the third. The middle is clear.

The station vibrates and the dark tunnel lights up. Fear of missing the train and having to wait on the platform in the stifling heat gets the heart racing and you scamper down the clear left-side of the escalator. Two women stand side-by-side and talk, stopping progress. They pause, look up at you and then back down the clear passage. They continue their conversation. "Excuse me, ma'am," you say with a light tap.

She looks perplexed, borderline annoyed, at the interruption and takes her time to move. "Can you believe him? He should have left earlier and not have to rush," she tells her friend as you sprint to the bottom.

The minute the metro doors open a scrum breaks out. Riders storm in and push back those struggling to get out. All the action takes place at the first car. At the second, a solitary, bald, portly man waits for people to get off, making it the better entry point and you bulldoze through the exiting commuters to get there.

The man steps in, turns, stops and crosses his arms over his belly. He has no intention of moving. The train beeps and powers to a start. Lowering the shoulder, you barge in just as the doors slide close. The man is full of hostility and his small brown eyes glare in anger. Paying him no mind, you step into a car that is far from full and see an open seat by a window.

The train jerking and swerving down the track makes walking a test of balance. The two ladies sit on the outside chairs, the inside ones used for their bags of recently bought clothes. Gossiping about the Princess of Spain's supposed eating disorder, they are oblivious to all those around and make little effort to accommodate those needing seats. Your solution to the problem is a light bump of the knees and quick step on the toes. They stop talking and take their belongings from the seat as you sit to a thud. They then resume their conversation.

In the middle of the aisle stands a man who continues to stare as if you're his dead uncle who has come back to life. People in most countries don't do that unless they want to get punched. Here, it is the norm. Over his shoulder is a young guy with a white-painted face. He whips out a large skeleton puppet from a black duffel bag and flips the switch to an old dusty radio. Gypsy music and fiddles blast from the speakers as he prances down the aisle, *the Nightmare Before Christmas* looking puppet singing and dancing to the rhythmic music. Kids start clapping and shouting, "*Olé, olé, olé! Ooooooooleeeeé!*" Soon everyone joins to create a chorus that rattles the walls and windows of the rumbling train.

The fading music has many reaching in their purses and wallets for loose change as the train slows to a stop. It no longer vibrates. Those leaving give the performer coins and wait by the opening doors. People storm in and people struggle out, all the while the bald portly man with crossed arms vigilantly guards the door.

***

Bursting out at the next stop, you're eager to get above ground. A congregating group of Spaniards discussing where to go next blocks the platform. A metal bench provides an unconventional way around. You hop on the wide plank to pass before jumping down in front of a middle-aged man who manages the complex feat of walking and reading at the same time. Leaning on the moving railing, you let the escalator do its job and stop rushing. All of the running around, crowds, stress, and failure to accomplish the simplest of tasks can leave even the most patient person feeling exhausted and frustrated. A girl on her way down smiles as if to say, that's how you do it. The rumble of the next train drowns out the sound of your lighter hitting the ground as you take out the ticket to pass through empty the turnstiles and continue up the stairs.

Above ground, the blasting beeps from the cars at a red light pound your head. A mustached man in a white van lays on his horn, leans out the window and shouts at the top of his lungs, "I shit on your whore of a mother! Fuck! Come on, cunt! I'm in a hurry." It's not clear who he's yelling at, the car in front, the red-light or Gaudí's ghost. But, he's not alone. The street erupts into an explosion of horns and shouts that jackhammer into your brain. It's easy to hate this city sometimes. A tap on the shoulder belongs to a young girl who holds out a lighter. She is blond with olive skin and brown eyes and wears a navy dress. "You dropped this," she says in Spanish.

"Oh, *gracias*."

"*De nada*. You look lost."

"Just wandering around and killing time before lunch."

"Are you visiting?"

"No, I live here."

"Really? I'm meeting some friends. Do you want to join us?"

If you had to sum up the Spanish and Catalans in two words, it'd be hospitable and non-cynical which in turn has made you more friendly and open. "Um, sure, why not?"

***

"Here we are." She stops at a wrought-iron door whose bars are bent into the outline of flowers in a vase. She buzzes and two seconds later, she steps into a sunny stone entryway. Looking up to the glass roof, you count seven stories and no elevator. "Come on. It's only on the third floor," she says walking up the first flight of short and worn steps to the *entresuelo.*

Not as tall as the other stories of Spanish buildings, the low ceiling of the landing forces your head to duck as you pass what appears to be two flats suitable only for housing midgets. The next set of steps leads to *la planta principal,* or the principal floor, and it has no ceiling. One more story up is *la planta primera* or the first floor. And that's when you hear it – the sputtering, spinning and wheezing of a drill. The girl sees the look of agitation on your face and says, "Don't worry, just two more flights."

The bar is a converted flat. Card-tables and folding chairs line walls decorated with local art. The smell of fried eggs, potatoes and fish wafts from the kitchen, making your empty stomach roar. At the end of the hall open glass-doors lead to a patio that offers a sense of space amid the surrounding congestion of the city. More importantly, there's no more drilling. "*Hola,*" says the girl to a middle-aged man behind the makeshift plywood bar.

"*Hola guapa,*" he replies and the two of you stroll past people of all ages sitting at the plastic tables. Loud talk and laughter fill the air and the birds sing in the branches of the trees that dot the patio. At the far back, a group of young people smile and wave enthusiastically to come over.

A round of quick pecks on each cheek for introductions and a skinny boy in a Vans t-shirt says, "Welcome."

"Hello. Thanks for having me."

"No thanks necessary here. We're Spanish and Catalans, not English. What do you want to drink – beer?"

"Sounds perfect."

The boy turns, raises his hand, and belts to the waiter, "Hey, come here!"

The man, who is old enough to be his father, strolls to the table. "What do you want?"

"More beer."

The waiter says nothing as he heads towards the makeshift bar, ignoring the couple with empty glasses and dirty plates trying to get his attention. The boy looks at you and says, "Where you from?"

"America."

"America?" The blond girl shrieks in horror. "I would never want to go there! I would much prefer to visit Australia; they are much more welcoming to foreigners."

You reply, "You think?"

"Have you ever tried to go Australia?" The boy in the Vans t-shirt comes to the U.S.'s defense. "You need a visa and the immigration officers don't speak any Spanish! All they like to do is get drunk and fight. They are like the English, but bigger and tanner."

"What the hell are you saying?" replies the girl. "At least they don't have Bush."

"But he's not the president anymore. Now they have Obama!"

"So you're American?" asks a prematurely balding man in a Ramones t-shirt and black square glasses.

Turning away from the heated discussion about which is better, America or Australia, being waged by two Spaniards, you say, "Yes."

"I went to Boston once."

"Did you like it?"

"Yes. I like English music, especially Bruce Springsteen, U2, Pearl Jam. I hate heavy metal."

"That's great."

"Do you know Spain very well?"

A pause as the waiter arrives with bottles of beer and leaves.

"Yeah, I've been to Andalucia, Pais Vasco and Asturias."

"Do you like it here?"

"Yeah. Each city is different and unique and the people are friendly and welcoming."

"We like to party, no?"

"That you do. How do you know everybody?"

"We all went to high-school together, some of us since elementary school."

"Wow."

"Yes. We meet here every other Saturday. I like this place." He stops as the waiter arrives with a stack of plates that he sets at the edge of the table. "You like Spanish food?"

"Yes."

"It's better than American food, no?"

"It depends. You eat a lot of fried food."

"Yes. But we use oil and not butter. But enough talk. Now, it's time to eat."

One waiter brings a fold-out table that he places next to yours and leaves. A second waiter arrives with massive round pan full of yellow rice topped with unpeeled prawns and crayfish, shelled mussels and clams, diced squid, cuttlefish and tomatoes that he places on the new table. A third waiter arrives with plates of cured ham, sliced blood sausages and toasted bread rubbed with fresh tomatoes and garlic. *"Bon profit,"* the two waiters say and leave.

"Eat, eat." The boy in the Ramones t-shirt hands you a plate.

"Thanks."

"Man, no thanks necessary here. This is not England. There, everyone is too polite. The say please, thank you and sorry even when they are bumping and pushing you."

You laugh.

He piles his plate with paella and then goes for the ham. "Do you know the secret of a good paella?"

"No." You take some sausage, ham, bread and rice, leaving the unpeeled seafood for the professionals after having come home too many times with more fish juice on your hands than meat in your stomach.

"Patience with the rice."

"I see."

Pa amb tomàquet is a Catalan staple and served with almost all meals. The toasted bread placates your hungry stomach while the tomato rubbed on it moistens your palate with a garlic bite. The boy was right about the rice - soft and sticky without even the slightest of crunch - your first mouthful brings with it the salty flavors of the sea and a memory of last weekend at the beach with friends. Most of the conversation takes place in rapid fire Spanish with a sprinkling of Catalan, making it easy to lose track of the shifting topics, people and locations. Your mind wanders to the serendipitous twists life in Barcelona brings and a smile crosses your face. Surreal situations, the strange characters, the chance of each day surprising you in a city whose buildings give it the feel of a Gothic fairytale in the sun, they are what make all the frustration that comes with living in your strange adopted land bearable. Tragic at times, but always amusing, they are the reasons why you live in this city.

***

An hour later, the pan is empty save for a few kernels of rice and the peeled shells of the seafood. The plates are gone and sleepiness sets in with rush of blood to your bloated stomach. A picture of an unmade double bed with two pillows flashes. *Proper siesta* minus one hour and counting. "That was good, no?" asks the young girl, her argument about Australia versus America long over.

"Yes, Thanks for inviting me."

"Enough with the please and thank you."

"Okay." You need to move and stand. Looking at the group of strangers sitting at the table and talking, you smile in appreciation for turning this into a great morning. "Thanks for having me. It's been a real pleasure." It's difficult not to be polite.

The young girl reprimands the cultural error with a scolding look.

"Sorry... I mean, I gotta get going. How much do I owe?" You count off a couple of twenties.

The boy in the Ramones t-shirt says, "Don't worry, man. It's on us."

"That's very kind. But seriously." You toss money on the table. "Thanks again for a great time. It was a pleasure to meet you all."

The boy stuffs the cash back in your pocket. "Please, don't worry. Keep the money. Just remember that not all Catalans are cheap."

"Don't worry. I know. And just remember - not all Americans are George Bush."

The girl who brought you laughs.

Four o'clock on a Saturday afternoon is the quietest time of the day in Barcelona. Most shops are closed and the streets are less congested as the city's residents finish their lunch. The shaded square across from the flat is empty and there's not even the faintest drilling in the white lobby. Drunk with food and buzzed from beer, you smile at the image of a waiting bed and stagger into the elevator. Back in the room, there are no beeps, shouts or bangs. The unmade bed with two soft pillows waits like a loving wife after a long trip and the siesta-count down stops. Shutting the blinds to introduce complete darkness, you crawl under the thin sheet and close your eyes, drifting to sleep to the rarest of sounds in Barcelona: silence.

Other Books on Barcelona

The Shadow of the Wind, Carlos Ruiz Zafón, 0753820250

The Angel's Game, Carlos Ruiz Zafón, 0753826496

The Colour of a Dog Running Away, Richard Gwyn, 1902638727

Home to Barcelona: A Foreigner's Story, Richard Manchester, 8447710246

My Christina and Other Stories, Merce Rodoreda, 0915308657

Cathedral by the Sea, Ildefonso Falcones, 0552773972

Homage to Barcelona, Colm Tóibín, 0330373560

Barcelona, Robert Hughes, 1860468241

Homage to Catalonia, George Orwell, 0141183055

Barça: A People's Passion, Jimmy Burns, 1408805782

About Jeremy Holland

Jeremy Holland was born near Los Angeles California but he didn't grow up there. His formative years were instead spent in the Saudi Arabia and a seaside town in England until life brought him back to the United States as a teenager. By his early twenties, he had returned to Los Angeles following a period living just outside of Washington D.C. and settled into a career working in technology after a succession of jobs and time spent at university. Surrounded by close family and friends, his life seemed complete but there was always a little voice in his head urging him to seek out new adventures in exotic lands and it was joined by a whisper suggesting he try to be a writer.

By the 2001 the whisper had turned into a roar and following a trip to Barcelona, he decided it was time to leave his life in the states, search out a new adventure and – like Hemingway, Gwyn, Toibin and Orwell before him – move to Spain to become a writer. Arriving in 2002 with a blanket, a laptop and just enough Spanish to order a beer, he set out to make a new life in his adoptive home where he continues to live and speak the language more or less – the city and its people inspiring a collection of short stories From Barcelona Vol. 1. He is also a regular contributor to the leading online expatriate news paper Expatica.com and a short story of his can be found in the inaugural edition of Barcelona INK.

For fiction, articles and features on Barcelona, Los Angeles and Expat Life get in touch...
Email: *jeremyholland@frombarcelona.com*
Visit: *www.frombarcelona.com*

Also available from
www.nativespain.com

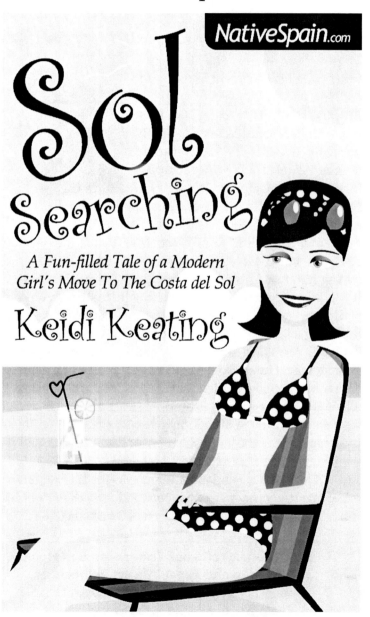

NativeSpain.com

Sol
searching

A Fun-filled Tale of a Modern
Girl's Move To The Costa del Sol

Keidi Keating

Also available from
www.nativespain.com

NativeSpain.com

Going Native in
Catalonia

Simon Harris

the essential guidebook for the inquisitive explorer